Ashley Sherer

The
Incredible Adventures
of
Jake Astro
Volume I

Ashley Sherer

Ashley Sherer

ISBN:0692331913
ISBN-13:978-0692331910

Ashley Sherer

To Katherine and Taylor, whom I love and whose spending habits gave me the time to finish my book.

To Tena, whose love and encouragement gave me the ability to finish what I started.

To Drew, Danny, and Alex, whom I wish all the success in the world.

Finally, thank you to everyone else who played a role in this book, from proofreading or advice or an encouraging word.

Cover photography by : www.facebook.com/photosbydeedee

Cover design by: www.fiverr.com/vikncharlie

Ashley Sherer

Ashley Sherer

CONTENTS

Ashley Sherer

Jake Astro
and the
Missing Professor

The
Mystery of the Ancients
Trilogy
Part I

Ashley Sherer

Ashley Sherer

"Excuse me, are you Captain Astro?"

"You're late," answered the man without looking up from his drink.

"I'm sorry about that, but this bar isn't the easiest place to find. I'm Zedra Naken," she said as she extended her hand.

Jake looked up from the thick green alcohol he had been drinking and about fell out of his chair. In sharp contrast to the dank, smoke filled bar, stood a statuesque blond. She was a vision standing six feet tall and wore shorts that allowed an almost disgraceful view of a set of perfect legs.

"No problem at all. Please have a seat," replied Jake as he ignored her outstretched hand.

"Thank you," Zedra replied as she sat down in the chair opposite of Jake.

"Would you like something to drink? Perhaps a spring water or a fruit juice?" offered Jake as he waived a waitress over through the teaming mass of humans, aliens, and well, no one's sure what else.

"I'll have what you're having."

"Are you sure? This is jangu and it's pretty strong."

Zedra picked up Jake's glass and drank it in one gulp.

"Not bad," she said as she licked her lips.

Zedra slammed the glass onto the table upside down.

"Two jangu," said Jake to the waitress, who nodded and walked back to the bar.

"Your friend Ram's description of you didn't do you justice," she said.

"Ram Achok isn't a friend. He's an underhanded, crooked middleman that would cut his mother's throat for an extra one percent commission."

"He said I should look for a tall, handsome, brown haired man with a dimpled chin and blue eyes."

"Ram always did have excellent eyesight," said Jake breaking into a slight grin.

"He should have added that you have a nice smile and broad shoulders."

"Thanks," said Jake as the waitress sat two glasses of jangu on the table, "but we should talk about what I can do for you."

"Oh, I'm sure you could do a lot, but my most immediate need is finding my father."

"Let's hear it Ms. Naken."

"Call me Zedra."

"Ok, Zedra. What's your story?"

"My father is Professor Arthur Naken. He's an archeologist that specializes in extremely ancient civilizations."

"Define extremely ancient."

"Civilizations whose existence is measured in the millions of years. He was leading an expedition in the jungles of Vega Onias based on carvings he had found on Esteon Three. My father had been there for about six weeks and had made three preliminary excursions into an area near the only established town on the planet. For the first four weeks, I heard from him like clockwork every other day. He would send me reports on his progress that I would analyze. Two weeks ago, everything stopped. There were no reports or any other contact. I want you to go in and find him."

Jake Astro leaned closer trying to read the expression of the mysterious blond woman seated in front of him.

"Can you help me, Captain Astro?"

"Please, it's Jake. Didn't your father have help or were these one-man expeditions?"

"He did have help, but I've not heard from them either."

Jake sighed, "Then why not call in the local law? This seems like something right up their alley."

Zedra crossed her legs and leaned in even further so that a whisper of jasmine wafted across Jake's nose.

"Well Jake," she purred, "my father is always willing to bend the rules with whatever he's searching for. As you might imagine, the local authorities don't always appreciate his methods and aren't inclined to help when he gets in trouble. Jake, I need your help. I can't imagine losing him."

Jake crossed his arms as he leaned back against the chair.

"Well, there's one small complication. I'm coming off probation from the galactic Gestapo. If I do anything the least bit shady, I'll lose my ship. No ship, no money."

"But I need you and I don't know where else to turn."

Tears welled up in the corner of her eyes as she bit her bottom lip.

"Fine, but it will cost you twenty thousand credits. Ten thousand now, and the rest when we find your father."

"Done."

A look of surprise flashed on Jake's face.

"Something wrong, Jake?"

"You seem to have recovered from your emotional breakdown rather quickly. I think I should have asked for more money."

"I'm desperate and you're my only hope. I will do anything to find my father."

"Meet me in hangar 34 at the spaceport with the ten thousand credits in one hour. Then I'll be on my way."

"We'll be on OUR way."

"Whoa," said Jake as he threw up his hands, "It's just me and Mikja."

"Mikja?"

"My partner."

"How intimate..." a sly smile crossed her lips as she stood.

Jake stood and leaned over the table.

"*Business* partner and co-pilot. By the way, the twenty thousand doesn't include being insulted."

"Jake, I'm sorry. I guess I'm abrasive when I'm under stress. I shouldn't have made a joke about your partner. That said, if you want the money, you'll take me with you."

Jake didn't like working with strangers, but this was the first job that had come his way since his probation had ended.

"Alright Ms. Naken, but get in my way or slow me down and I'll park you on the nearest asteroid WITHOUT a spacesuit."

Zedra stood up and walked over to Jake. She grabbed him by his shirt and pulled him close.

"I won't be in the way, and I think you'll find that you have to keep up with me."

Zedra pressed her soft lips against Jake's and kissed him. Without a word, she turned and walked out of the bar. Jake stumbled over the table as he sat back down into his chair. It had been a long time since he had been kissed that way and never by anyone who looked as stunning as Zedra.

"Whew, maybe this job won't be so bad after all," Jake said to himself.

Jake pulled out his communicator and punched the code to call his ship.

"Get everything fired up, we leave in an hour."

"Did we get it?" a high-pitched voice replied.

"We've got it. Straighten up the place, we'll be taking a passenger."

"She was attractive wasn't she?" asked the voice.

"Mikja, she's paying us twenty thousand credits. I think that would make your grandmother attractive."

"You didn't answer the question."

"Yes, she is attractive. Happy?"

"Extremely. I'll have the ship ready."

Jake put the communicator back into his pocket and walked outside. The jangu had made him forget why he hated this particular bar. It was right beside the town's marketplace and it was crowded today. Every three steps, some toothless merchant accosted Jake by trying to sell him everything from home remedies that stank like a decaying corpse to unidentifiable fried animals. The patrons were even worse. Their aroma made the home remedies smell like a fine perfume. After three collisions, one near fistfight and a slight dousing of something that smelled like rancid milk, Jake reached the spaceport. In front of the entrance gate, a short, fat, balding man in a blue uniform stood watch.

"Got some ID, space jockey?" asked the guard.

"Yeah, hold on. I've got it somewhere. And that's Mr. Space Jockey to you," said Jake as he went through his pockets.

"Come on, I haven't got all day," replied the guard as he held out his hand and tapped his foot in frustration.

"Here it is, sunshine."

"Watch your lip and get in there," said the guard as he jerked his thumb toward the entrance.

Jake strolled through the metal door into the building, and hopped on the moving walkway. When he reached hangar 34, Jake stepped off and went up to the metal security door. Beside the door was a small black numeric keypad.

"6-2-3-5-1-5," Jake said to himself as he punched in the key code to open the door.

"Access Denied, please try again," the voice from the keypad informed.

Jake tried once more, "6-2-3-5-1-5."

"Access Denied, please try again," the voice repeated.

Jake banged on the door and screamed, "Mikja let me in! You better not have changed the code again!"

After a few more minutes of banging, the door slid open.

"Sorry Captain."

"Why did you change the code?"

"They're out to get us and I didn't want us end up in a prison camp or worse."

"Exactly, who is out to get us?"

"They are."

Jake had learned it was best not to question his competent, but paranoid, co-pilot.

"I'm going to run the final preflight checks," said Mikja as he walked up the ramp.

"I'll finish the external inspection," yelled Jake.

The Obsidian had served him well, but was an older

model of starship and needed a little extra care. It had been 10 years since Jake had 'acquired' his baby. At 50 feet in diameter with a height of 30 feet, it was the perfect ship for the small, custom cargo jobs he took to make his living. As he walked around the ship, the pitted and scarred black exterior plating reminded him of the all the tight spots she had been through. When the inspection was finished, Jake paused and patted the main engine.

"Come on girl, let's get ready for one more ride."

A smile crossed his face as he walked up the ramp and joined Mikja in the cockpit.

"She's late, Captain."

"Be patient Mikja, she IS a woman."

"A very hot woman apparently."

"Apparently," Jake echoed as he drummed his fingers on the control panel.

"She might not show," said Mikja.

"How long have we been working together, about three years?", Mikja nodded, "Have I ever been wrong about a client?"

"I better not answer that if I want to make it another three years."

Jake sighed as he glanced at the ship's chronometer to see that Zedra was 15 minutes late.

"Do you think she cooks her food?" asked Mikja.

"Yes, I think so. She's human, so I would assume she cooks her food."

"Oh well, what a shame. By the way, did you warn her that I was a Lacertilian?"

"I thought it was best to not tell her."

"Really? You thought it was best for her to be confronted by a six foot tall green lizard."

"I did. And you're really more of an olive color," said Jake with a broad grin on his face.

"You're a mean man, Captain," replied Mikja with a smile on his face.

"Yep. Consider it a test of her interstellar familiarity."

"I knew there was a reason I liked working with you."

As the two continued to talk, a loud banging came from the hangar door.

"That should be her. I'll go let her in," said Jake.

"I think I'll come with you."

Jake walked to the hangar door, with Mikja trailing behind, and pressed a green button by its side. As he did, the door slid open.

"You can't afford a hangar with a working intercom?" asked Zedra as she walked into the room and toward the Obsidian.

"Sorry, your highness. I'll do better next time."

Zedra turned from wildcat to kitten in the blink of an eye, as she threw her arms back around Jake.

"I'm sorry Jake, I'm just so worried about my father."

Jake enjoyed the embrace for somewhat longer than he should have before he pulled away and led her onto the ship.

"Zedra, I'd like you to meet Mikja," said Jake as he stepped aside to reveal his co-pilot who was standing by him.

"A Lacertilian? This is a rare pleasure indeed. I have always wanted to meet a member of such a fascinating people."

"Why thank you. The pleasure is all mine and Jake's description of you certainly didn't do you justice."

"You two stop the love fest and strap in. We'll be taking off in five minutes. Zedra, you take this seat," said Jake as he motioned toward a seat near the front of the ship directly behind the cockpit.

Zedra sat down in the chair and snapped on her safety harness.

"Ahh, fine Corinthian leather," commented Zedra as she ran her fingers over seat.

"Princess, I suggest that you don't make fun of my ship. She's a classic that has a lot of life left in her. She's equipped with a null gravity generator and a hyperspace curve drive. More importantly, she's gotten me out of more sticky situations than I can count."

"So a number larger than 11?" asked Zedra.

"You know, I'm not superstitious, but I think she's got a mind of her own. It'd be sad if you got flushed into space when hitting the head," said Jake.

The color drained from Zedra's face as she sat back into her chair.

"I'll keep that in mind," she gulped.

Jake went back up to the front of the ship where Mikja was going through his final preflight responsibilities.

"Not a word or you're luggage."

"You know that's why we were created right. We were genetically engineered for luggage," said Mikja.

Jake shook his head, "One of these days, I'll learn."

"No you won't, humans were genetically engineered for stupidity."

"You made that one up," complained Jake.

Mikja turned back without a word and continued with the preflight preparations.

"Control, this is Jake Astro of the Obsidian, please open the outer hangar doors. We are ready for departure."

"Roger Obsidian," replied the voice from the control tower.

Ashley Sherer

The hangar doors slid open as a robot tow tractor rolled without a sound beside the Obsidian. A massive robot arm extended and grabbed a tow hook on the back of the ship. The tractor rolled out of the hangar and onto the launch pad with the Obsidian in tow. Once in place, the tractor released the ship and moved away. When the tractor had retreated to a safe distance, the engines of the Obsidian started to hum and emit a soft white glow.

"Activate the null gravity field."

Mikja flipped a green switch on the control panel and the ship slowly floated upwards.

"Fire rockets."

The engines kicked in with a slight jolt and the Obsidian zoomed skyward. Billowy white clouds gave way to clear blue sky until the cockpit viewport showed the deep blackness of space.

"We have exited the atmosphere and entered orbit. I'm disengaging the rockets, Captain."

The rocket engines of the Obsidian dimmed as the ship's acceleration slowed.

"You ok back there princess?"

The slight green tinge on the face of Zedra answered Jake's question better than any words could.

"I guess you're not used to traveling off world on a ship that uses a null gravity generator?"

"No, I had no idea that ships still used that. It's

21

practically ancient."

Jake's face curled up in disgust. No one talked about the Obsidian except him. And Mikja. And that one guy on Rigel 4. Well, not this spoiled little rich girl.

"Not everyone can afford to get a new ship every year."

Zedra bent over holding her stomach.

"Not in the mood to talk? That's probably for the best, but don't worry about it. The sickness will pass in a few hours. I've heard the key to a quick recovery is remaining calm and quiet."

Jake turned back to Mikja.

"Are you going to tell her about the null gravity sickness pills?" asked Mikja.

"Nope."

"Good call, although remember it's your turn to clean up the mess. Also, the computer has plotted the hyperspace curve and we're ready to go when you give the word."

"Let's get her highness to her appointed destination."

Mikja entered the command into the computer and the ship vibrated slightly. As the vibrations increased in intensity, the ship became translucent and entered the hyperspace curve. Jake couldn't describe the experience when riding the hyperspace curve to anyone. You had to experience it. It was like riding a rainbow that included every color and hue in the visible light spectrum and Jake never grew tired of it. After three hours of mostly silent travel, a red light blinked rapidly on the control panel.

"What's that? Is something wrong?" came the weak voice from the back of the ship.

"I knew the silence was too good to last," said Jake as he leaned close to Mikja.

As Mikja laughed, Jake turned his chair back toward the rear of the ship.

"It's just the warning light to let us know we're approaching our destination. We'll be in orbit around Vega Onias in ten minutes."

Jake took a small package from the front pocket of his shirt and tossed it back to Zedra.

"Here take this. It'll help with the null gravity sickness."

Zedra looked up from holding her stomach, "You son of a-"

"You're wasting time when you could be taking the medicine."

Zedra opened the packet and gulped down the contents as Jake turned around. The ship shuddered slightly as it came out of the hyperspace curve.

"Mikja, contact the Vega Onias spaceport and let them know we're coming in for a landing. I'm going back to talk with Zedra."

"Roger, Skipper."

Jake undid his harness strap and moved to the back of the ship where Zedra had isolated herself.

"That was a dirty trick you played on me, not giving me those null gravity sickness pills."

"Yep."

"Yep? No apology?" asked Zedra.

"Nope."

"Why did you come back here?"

"We need to get our game plan set. Where's the bar at this spaceport?"

Zedra grabbed Jake's arm and pulled him toward her.

"Are you serious? You're worried about finding a drink?"

"Yes, because it'll be me and nothing but glorious alcohol there. No one that might work in those jungles or have any information ever goes to a bar."

Jake pulled his arm free and glared at Zedra.

"I'm sorry, I wasn't thinking. It's just to the south of the spaceport. This is a small colony, there's only the one."

Jake ignored her apology and continued, "We hit the bar, and I'll discreetly ask a few questions. Maybe someone there has seen your dad or maybe if we're lucky we'll find your father's assistants."

Zedra laid her hand on top of Jake's and the warmth felt good to him.

"Thank you. I'm sorry for being so much trouble."

Zedra and Jake drew closer together, her finger resting gently on his chin.

"Captain, we're cleared for landing!"

"Perfect timing," sighed Jake.

Jake turned back toward Zedra.

"We'll continue this later," said Jake.

"Count on it," said Zedra as a suggestive smile crept on her face.

Jake walked back to the cockpit and took his place in the captain's chair. After navigating the ship down through the atmosphere, Jake landed the Obsidian on the concrete pad at the Vega Onias spaceport.

"Mikja, stay with the ship. Zedra and I are going to poke around and see if we can learn anything."

"No problem, you know what they say about this planet anyway?"

"I'm almost afraid to ask, but what do they say?"

"The rumor is that this planet was terraformed by some terrorist group when they were testing a planet killer weapon. This was just a regular uninhabited world with different temperate zones. When the weapon was set off, instead of causing a massive atomic reaction, it somehow caused a massive energy release that covered the entire planet in thick jungle foliage. It's also why there's a lot of seismic activity. The whole place is going to blow up one day."

"Or it could just be a jungle world that has earthquakes. That does happen," Jake replied.

"That's what they want you to believe."

Jake knew that any conspiracy discussion with Mikja would consume the rest of the day and most of the night, so he let his last remark go without a comeback.

"Is your co-pilot always so paranoid?" asked Zedra.

"He'd tell you that it's not paranoia if they really are out to get you."

Jake and Zedra walked down the ramp of the ship and approached a short, stout man standing on the edge of the landing pad holding a small computer pad.

"Morning," said Jake.

"Are you Captain Jake Astro?" asked the man, not looking up from his computer.

"I am."

"I'm Vargo Jenkins and I just need to take care of a few things before you get going. If I can get 500 credits and your bio-scan, we can let you get on with your business."

Jake pulled a card from out of his pocket and gave it to the man who slid it through a slot on his computer pad.

"Thank you Mr. Astro, it seems like everything is in order. Have a pleasant stay on Vega Onias," said Vargo as he gave the card back to Jake.

"Ready to get started, Zedra?" asked Jake.

"I am, but I didn't think the spaceport would meet you on the pad. I thought you had to go into the office and take care of all the formalities."

"He's not with the spaceport. Let's just say he's part of a certain segment of the population that likes to 'protect' your ship while you're here," said Jake as he shrugged his shoulders.

"You mean he's a criminal."

"Not exactly. He's part of the local 'protection' guild. It's how business is done on these 'less traveled' worlds. Let me run into the office and I'll get the official stuff taken care of."

Jake was in the spaceport office for only a few minutes before he came back out and met up with Zedra.

"Any problems?" she asked.

"Nope, and as a plus I got directions to the bar."

"Lead the way."

The two walked south along the street heading away from the spaceport. After a few hundred yards, they came to a large dilapidated wooden building with a large neon sign hanging over the main entrance. The strong smell of alcohol, sawdust, and bile wafted through the air. As they stood and watched, they saw the outline of several humanoids stagger out into the night air and down the street.

"Do I even want to know what that sign says?" asked Zedra.

"In any language princess, it spells 'dump'. Wait out here. I'll go in and do the talking."

"Be my guest," said Zedra as she waved Jake by.

A wave of silence swept the room as Jake walked into the bar and all eyes fell on him. He made his way around the room trying to glean information about the professor with little success until he felt a tap on his shoulder. As he turned around, Jake stared into the muscular green chest of the largest humanoid he had ever seen. It was eight feet tall with a human-like face and a heavy ridged brow. All four of the incisor teeth were at least two inches long and looked as if they could tear through his flesh with no effort. The brute was dressed largely in gray animal fur with leather straps holding a long bladed weapon and a knife around his waist. Jake wouldn't have been surprised if it had killed everything it wore.

"Hi friend," said Jake as he raised his hand in what he hoped would be recognized as a sign of friendship.

Without warning, the beast swung his left fist, narrowly missing Jake's head. Jake threw his best punch straight into what he hoped were the creature's ribs but it was like hitting a concrete wall.

"Owwwwwwww," Jake yelled.

Jake grabbed his hand as the giant's hand swung toward him, this time connecting with his shoulder. The wind was knocked out of Jake as he was picked up by his injured shoulder and leg. With no visible effort, it walked to the door and hurled Jake 15 feet through the air and out into the street. As the beast walked outside, the crowd in the bar began to follow until it turned toward them and growled fiercely, baring its fangs. As if on cue, the group sat back down and didn't make a move toward the door. The creature continued out into the street until it stood over Jake's still prone body. The heavy sound of footsteps approaching brought Jake out of the haze he was in.

"Listen friend, I don't know what I did but," mumbled Jake trying to focus on the beast standing over him.

Bending down, the creature snatched Jake up by his leg and held him upside down so that Jake was face to face with his monstrous antagonist.

"Please be quiet and pretend you're unconscious. I have news for you and your female friend about the professor. She's already been taken to our destination."

The soft voice belied the mammoth hulk that had manhandled him. Jake closed his eyes and hoped he wasn't making a mistake trusting this huge behemoth. Carrying Jake like he was weightless, they bounded across the street and through alleyways until they came to the edge of town. From there, he ran through the jungle, holding Jake under his left arm, until they came to a campfire encircled by three tents. Jake was surprised when he saw Zedra and a similar creature sitting around the campfire talking and laughing like two old friends who hadn't seen each other for years. However, Zedra's new colleague was different than the one that toted him. The curves that were accented by the flickering firelight made it clear that this one was a female.

"Glad you could make it Jake, we've just been talking about you."

The female creature made a noise that Jake hoped was laughter, although it sounded more like a cat being strangled. The male creature lowered Jake gently to the ground and brushed him off.

"I apologize for the brusque behavior earlier. Your questions had marked you for a beating or worse."

Jake grimaced as he felt his ribs and tried to move his fingers on his injured left hand.

"Apology accepted; although I wish you had given me some warning. I think I've got a few cracked ribs and if my hand isn't broken it's a miracle."

"We have a healing ray provided by the professor that should take care of such minor things. Allow me to introduce myself, my name is Rheylaash, and this is my life mate Qazjix. We're from the planet Wixila."

Jake extended his right hand and the creature shook it.

"Jake Astro. Now that formal introductions are complete, how about that healing ray?"

"Come with me and remove your shirt."

Jake and Rheylaash walked over to a small metal case next to the campfire. Rheylaash opened the case and pulled out a gray metal cube about the size of an apple as Jake took off his shirt.

Zedra whispered something to Qazjix as they looked at Jake and both laughed.

"See something you like, Zedra?"

Zedra shook her head and laughed, "You flatter yourself."

"Just a few days ago, you were purring over me like a kitten. Why you little-"

"Jake," interrupted Rheylaash, "the ray should accelerate your body's natural healing ability. Within 12 hours, you should be completely healed."

As Rheylaash flipped a small switch on the side, a greenish-yellow light emanated from the front of the cube. Rheylaash moved the light slowly across Jake's ribs and hand. After about 20 seconds, Rheylaash flipped the switch again and the light went out.

"One treatment should be all you need."

"Thank you," said Jake as he slipped his shirt back on.

"Wait, do you hear that?" said Rheylaash as he looked at Qazjix.

"Brace yourselves," ordered Qazjix.

"What, I don't hear..." a low rumble interrupted Jake.

The sound grew louder and as it did, the ground started to shake. Jake and Rheylaash grabbed onto a nearby tree while Qazjix steadied Zedra. Then, as suddenly as the earthquake began, it stopped. For several seconds, the four remained silent, not knowing if the worst was over.

"Is that part of the treatment?" asked Jake with a smile on his face.

"No. Unfortunately, it is one of the less desirable features of this planet. Periodic earthquakes affect this region."

"Wonderful. Will you and Qazjix tell us what you know about the professor and the last time he was seen?"

Rheylaash gestured for Jake to sit down by the campfire and join Qazjix and Zedra.

"The professor had heard of ruins located north of here from a time before the planet was covered with jungle."

Jake made a mental note to tell Mikja that not all of his theories were crazy.

"Six weeks ago, Professor Naken hired the both of us as combination research assistants and laborers. For the next two weeks, we trekked through some of the most difficult and dangerous territory on the planet. Just before making camp for the night, the professor wanted to make a quick survey of a valley we had come upon. He suggested that we stay behind to set up camp as he went ahead. We didn't think there was any danger so we let him go. If we had only known what was going to happen..."

Zedra broke in. "It's alright, you had no idea."

"Thank you. We grew very fond of your father and his love of learning," said Rheylaash.

"Do you have any idea of what happened to him or where he could have disappeared to?" asked Jake.

"Unfortunately no. When he didn't come back to camp, we searched the valley for several days-"

"Why didn't you contact Zedra?" interrupted Jake.

"The professor had left strict instructions for us to not contact anyone in the event of an emergency," explained Qazjix, "He knew that Zedra would come and find him."

"What do you think we do now Jake?" asked Zedra.

"The valley is still our best bet. I'll get Mikja on the radio and ask him to meet up with us. He and I will then head out to the valley and see what we can find."

"You're not going without me," said Zedra.

"Or without Qazjix and I. We know the land and the people," said Rheylaash.

"Ok, but let's not try to advertise what we're doing to the whole world. Let me radio Mikja."

Jake pulled his radio out of his pocket.

"Mikja, do you read me?"

"I hear you Captain. What's up?"

"How's everything at the ship?"

"It's quiet. How's the town?"

"We've left the town and made camp in the jungle.
That's why I'm calling. I need you to bring the
supplies into town. When you get there, you'll meet
up with two Wixilans. Their names are Rheylaash
and Qazjix."

"How will I know them?"

"Look for the eight foot tall muscular green tinted
folk."

"Hmm, green, large and muscular. I wouldn't want
to get them angry, I don't think I would like them
when they get angry."

"That's an interesting perspective from someone who
is essentially a giant lizard. Just bring the stuff and
don't freak them out with any conspiracy talk."

"Captain, you know I can't keep the truth from being
exposed. If I did, I'd be as bad as them."

"Who are 'them'? Wait, never mind. Just not too
much talk, ok?"

"Ok, Captain. I promise."

Jake put the radio back in his pocket and turned to

Zedra.

"It could get dangerous out there. There's a lot about this world we don't know. If you want, you could stay here in the camp."

Zedra jabbed her finger into Jake's chest.

"I'll pretend you didn't say that. I've been in the field since I was six. When my mother died, I became my father's chief research assistant."

"I'm sorry to hear that. Not much of a childhood?"

"Actually, it was the best childhood anyone could ask for, new places and new things to explore constantly. Why me and dad once..."

Her voice trailed off as a single tear fell down her cheek.

Jake sat down beside Zedra and put his arm around her.

"Don't worry, we'll find him. I promise."

Jake leaned forward and kissed her, his hands cupping the sides of her face. Her soft skin felt good against his rugged hands. For a few minutes, the world slipped away, until Zedra pushed her hands against Jake's chest and stood up.

"Good night, Mr. Astro."

Zedra stood abruptly and went into her tent as Jake wondered what the hell had just happened. After he resigned himself to the fact that he would never understand women, Jake reclined against a fallen tree log and watched the stars until he fell asleep. Thanks to the effectiveness of the healing ray, Jake slept several hours until he felt a nudge against his arm and the foul stench of dead flesh wafted about his nostrils.

"Captain, wake up."

Jake jerked awake. The face of his co-pilot was about four inches from his.

"Mikja I've warned you not to do that. You know it wouldn't kill you to brush your teeth once in a while. Those live rats you eat make you smell like an open sewer."

"Captain, that toothpaste has fluoride. Everyone knows that fluoride is a chemical that lets them control a person's mind more easily."

"Great, mind control," said Jake as he threw up his arms.

"Glad you see it my way, captain."

"Wait, I..."

Jake thought better about engaging Mikja into another conspiracy discussion.

"We have all the supplies and should be ready to leave within the hour," interrupted Rheylaash much to Jake's relief.

"Has anybody woke up the princess?"

Zedra answered from behind Jake where she was taking down one of the tents.

"I've been up for an hour, jerk. One of us needed to start packing up our gear for the trip and your sleeping beauty butt wasn't going to do it."

Jake was amazed that the silky smooth demeanor from last night could turn to rough sandpaper in those few hours.

"I like to conserve my energy. By the way, it's your last chance to wait here at the camp."

"You can't keep me away," responded Zedra.

The ragtag search party gathered up their gear and set off on their journey into the valley. Rheylaash led with Qazjix by his side. The knowledge that anything that they would run into would have to face the two Wixilans first, gave Jake a good feeling. Jake, Zedra, and Mikja followed up behind them, watching so that nothing would sneak up from their rear. For the next several hours, the party went deeper and deeper into the jungle, hacking out a path with large machetes. Each step forward was a battle against vines and branches as thick as a man's leg.

"Rheylaash, I'm not saying that you're not doing a good job, but why aren't we going on the path that you and the professor took? It's taking us forever to cut through this jungle."

The giant alien laughed.

"We are on the path the professor and I cut, Jake Astro. You should have seen our trail when the professor and I were cutting it for the first time. These vines are what have grown back since our first excursion."

Jake sighed as the two Wixilan resumed cutting a trail for another hour when Zedra tapped Qazjix on the shoulder.

"I need to stop for a minute."

"Is everything ok?" asked Qazjix.

"I need a moment in private."

"A moment in private?" asked Mikja, "That's a strange human term."

"She has to pee," said Jake.

Zedra's face turned red.

"Yes, I need to pee, but thanks for letting the whole world know," said Zedra with her hands on her hips.

"Go ahead," said Jake.

Zedra crossed her arms and shook her head.

"You are sadly mistaken if you think I'm going to the bathroom right here in front of everyone. I'll just step off the trail a few feet and be right back."

"Be careful," said Qazjix.

Zedra took her machete and cut a small side trail about five feet away from the party.

"Can you see me?"

"No," replied Rheylaash.

"Eeeeeeeeeee!" cried Zedra.

"Zedra, that's not funny!" yelled Jake.

There was no reply from the brush.

"Zedra? Zedra! Everybody spread out, but be careful."

The search through the dense jungle started as they fanned out from the trail, checking for any sign of Zedra.

"Can you hear us?" yelled Jake.

"Jake?" came a faint voice.

"Zedra, where are you? I can barely hear you," said Jake as he knelt down.

"I don't know my feet went out from under me. I've fallen down some kind of pit."

"Are you hurt?"

"No, I think I'm ok."

"Keep talking, you're getting louder."

"Jake, over here. It's coming from this direction," said Qazjix.

Jake walked over to Qazjix who was about six feet from where the group had gone off the trail. As he searched the jungle ground, his left foot slipped out from under him.

"Whoa!" he yelled.

As Jake started to fall, his arms shot out and grabbed some of the dense brush that was everywhere in this jungle. After he steadied himself, Jake looked down where he slipped and pushed aside several green vines that ran along the ground.

"I've found a hole. Are you down there Zedra?"

"Yes, I can see you. I'm about 12 feet down."

"Don't be afraid, we'll be down to get you soon. It'll be just a few minutes till we're able to tie off a rope and come pull you up."

"Thanks Qazjix. I've got my flashlight. I want to see how big this hole is."

Jake took a rope from his backpack and tied it around a nearby tree. Testing its strength, he climbed down into the hole where Zedra's voice came from. Once on the ground, Jake turned on his flashlight and realized that it wasn't a hole that Zedra had fallen into, but a cave. Shining the beam around, Jake didn't see any trace of Zedra.

"Zedra?"

"Can you follow my voice and my flashlight, I need to show you something."

The cave was as warm as the jungle above and had the same dank decaying smell. The floors were lightly covered with a slick green slime that made walking around on oil-slicked ice seem tame. Jake moved cautiously and finally reached the part of the cave where Zedra was located.

"I hope you're happy, I nearly broke my neck getting over here."

Zedra shined her light against the wall.

"Look."

Jake leaned in to see that someone had carved a large arrow in the side of the cave pointing deeper into the tunnel.

"Ok, some kids came in here and carved an arrow."

Zedra lowered her flashlight and revealed to Jake that the initials 'A.N.' were carved into the wall.

"It's my father, he's been here."

Jake bent down and examined the initials closely. He ran his fingers over them and felt they were clean compared to the rest of the walls in the cave.

"I agree. Let's get the group down here and see what we can find."

Jake and Zedra walked back to where the entrance to the cave was located.

"Mikja, are you up there?" asked Jake.

"I am."

"We've found evidence of Zedra's father was down here. Bring all the gear down. The search continues from here."

"Will do," replied Mikja.

The three remaining members each climbed down the rope to the cave floor bringing all their equipment with them.

"This is quite the place you've found here, Captain"

"Thanks, with a little paint and some plants, it could grow on me."

"Paint?" asked Qazjix.

"Plants?" asked Rheylaash.

"Don't pay any attention to them, you two. It's the ramblings of little children," said Zedra.

"I'll ignore that for now," replied Jake.

"What's the plan, Captain?" asked Mikja.

"I'm not an expert like the princess over here, but I say we head in the direction of the arrow."

"You're right Jake, you're not the expert," snapped Zedra.

"Everyone take it nice and slow, these tunnels are slick. Also, watch the walls and see if we can find any more arrows," instructed Jake as he ignored Zedra.

With Jake and Zedra in the lead, they headed down the tunnel in the direction that the arrow indicated.

After walking 50 feet, Jake exclaimed, "Another arrow."

When he examined the arrow closer, he saw the

professor's initials carved below it, similar to the first arrow. As they kept going along the cavern, at various intervals, more arrows were found that indicated which way to go. The further into the tunnels they went, the temperature began to drop off dramatically.

"I wish we had brought jackets," complained Zedra.

"You know boss, this cold temperature isn't the best for me either."

"I know, we'll turn back if it gets much worse."

Jake turned toward Rheylaash and Qazjix.

"How are you two?"

"We are fine. Our genetic breeding allows us to withstand a wide temperature range. It will have to be a good bit colder before it starts to affect us," answered Rheylaash.

"Good, let's try to go a couple of more hours."

The group kept working their way down the tunnel for two more hours before Jake called a halt for rest.

"Break out the lunch and let's take five," said Jake.

"And where do you suggest we sit to enjoy this fine lunch," asked Zedra.

Jake picked up a rock and handed it to Zedra.

"Why don't you scrape the slime off these rocks and then we'll have a place to sit?"

To Jake's surprise, Zedra did just that and within a few minutes, the group was sitting in relative comfort. Rheylaash distributed the food and everyone ate with little conversation. Qazjix finished her food first and stood up.

"I'll scout ahead a bit while you rest."

Qazjix took her flashlight and walked down the tunnel until her light couldn't be seen. The group continued to eat for the next few minutes until a bouncing light could be seen coming from the tunnel that Qazjix was exploring. Jake grabbed his gun and raised it until he realized it was Qazjix running toward them. Jake had seen how strong the Wixilan were, but he was truly amazed at how a creature so big and strong could also be that fast and graceful.

"I've found something we all need to see. Follow me, but please stay quiet," said Qazjix not even out of breath from her run.

The group stood up and followed Qazjix down the tunnel. They had gone about 600 yards when she motioned for everyone to slow down and walk against the side of the tunnel. They continued this for another ten yards until coming to a pile of rocks that partially blocked the tunnel. Qazjix signaled for everyone to stay low and peer out over the rocks. The sight took Jake's breath away. Past the rocks, lay a huge cavern with what appeared to be an ancient stone city. Bioluminescent lichen, around the cavern and on the buildings, illuminated the area so that the flashlights were no longer needed.

"Wow, can you hand me the binoculars, Mikja?"

"Yeah, Captain."

Mikja opened the brown leather bag he was carrying and handed Jake a pair of scratched and gouged black binoculars. He looked through them and studied the city more closely. The buildings were made of the black stone that the cavern was made out of. They varied in size from one to three stories. Strange geometric symbols, which Jake assumed were some type of language, covered many of the buildings. Oddly, the slime that seemed to be present on the floor and walls of the tunnel wasn't present on any of the city structures. Empty streets cut through the buildings in a logical, well laid out pattern that would rival any modern planned city.

"Should we go down there?" asked Rheylaash

"It looks safe enough. I don't see anyone and it looks long deserted. Come on Rheylaash, let's take a look."

Jake and Rheylaash climbed over the rocks and down to the floor of the massive cavern. Not seeing any danger, they called for the others to join them. Once everyone was down, they walked over to the outer buildings of the city.

"Jake, do you see any more indicators anywhere?" asked Zedra.

"No, nothing. The whole place looks empty and deserted."

"Professor Naken! Are you here?" yelled Jake as they continued walking down what appeared to be the main street of the city.

Without warning, a sea of human-like figures flooded out of the buildings and surrounded the group.

Unlike any species Jake had seen, they made no shouts or battle cries, but remained silent with blank stares on their faces.

"What now Jake, do we fight?" asked Rheylaash.

Jake sized up these new creatures quickly. They were tall and muscular, a bit taller than an average sized human, but shorter than the Wixilan. They could have been cousins to the Wixilan, except for a few striking differences. The creatures' skin was ghostly white and their eyes were fiery pink with extremely large pupils. They carried long wooden spears and had black stone knives strapped to leather belts around their waists.

"No, don't resist," Jake ordered.

Out of the corner of his eye, Jake saw Qazjix start to raise her weapon. He quickly gestured for her to lower it. There were too many of these creatures to try to fight their way out without anyone being killed. One of the tallest creatures stepped forward. Without a word, he raised his spear and pointed to a small building 20 feet to the right of the group. The message was crystal clear.

"I guess he's the leader. Let's play along for now and go with them to that building."

"Like we have a choice," said Zedra.

"Just stay cool and nobody panic."

The group walked toward the building the tall creature had pointed to as all the creatures trailed behind them. Their destination was a small stone structure with a heavy wooden door. The leader pulled a key from a pouch around his waist and unlocked the door. He opened it and pointed with his spear inside. Without warning, Jake and the rest of the group were shoved in the room leaving them in darkness, as the door slammed shut.

"Who is it, who are you?" a weak voice called from the back of the room.

"Dad, is that you?"

Jake turned on his flashlight and swung the beam toward the voice, showing a bound figure lying in the corner of the room.

Zedra ran over to her father and hugged him tightly.

"Ugghh," Professor Naken groaned.

"I'm so sorry daddy, are you hurt?"

"Nothing serious, the Borrol just don't know their own strength."

Rheylaash walked over to the professor, knelt down, and cut his bonds loose.

"It's good to see you and Qazjix again. We have quite the party gathered."

"We are glad to see you as well, professor. So these creatures are called the Borrol?"

Naken rubbed his wrists and ankles.

"Yes, amazing species. Apparently, they live-"

"Daddy this is Jake Astro and his co-pilot Mikja. I

hired them to help find you," interrupted Zedra.

Jake stepped over and knelt down beside Naken.

"Good to meet you sir. We'll see if we can't get out of here and back to the surface. Can you stand?"

"I think so but I need a little help. I've been tied up for quite a while."

Jake extended his hand and helped Naken to his feet.

"Continue your story about all this, professor. How did you get down here and what else do you know about these Borrol as you called them?" said Jake.

The professor started to talk as he walked around to restore circulation to his limbs.

"I told Rheylaash and Qazjix that I wanted to scout around a bit in the valley before dark. They went to make camp while I pushed ahead. I walked around for about an hour before I decided to head back."

The professor placed his hand over his mouth and coughed. After he had cleared his throat, he continued.

"Sorry. I was just about to radio them and let them know I was on my way, when I stumbled into a hole. Luckily, I didn't break or sprain anything, but my radio wasn't as fortunate. I found it smashed from the fall. My flashlight survived, so I started to find a way out."

The professor paused and coughed again.

"I'm so sorry, I don't suppose you have any water?"

"Here you go professor," said Mikja as he pulled a small canteen from his bag.

The professor took a long drink and handed the canteen back to Mikja.

"Thank you. Now where was I? Oh yes, I remember. As I made my way into the tunnel, I scratched the arrows as a marker in case Rheylaash and Qazjix found the hole and came after me. Eventually, I came to the cavern and found the lost city. I had just started looking over the markings on the buildings when I was overwhelmed. They tied me up and threw me in here. For the last week, they've kept me in here letting me out only for brief stretches of time and feeding me the most distasteful mixture."

"I guess it kept you alive though," interrupted Zedra.

"Yes, whatever it was, it did keep me alive."

"Now how do you know they these are the Borrol, they didn't seem like they had any spoken language?" asked Jake.

"They don't. You see these Borrol, were genetically bred to be workers."

"Bred by who and to work on what?"

"Mikja, isn't it?"

Mikja nodded.

"They were bred to do all the manual work of the civilization that built this city. By who, I'm not sure.

I was able to study the city and the markings on my brief trips out of this room. The symbols are similar to some on Gamma 12, so I was able to piece together some of their meaning. On one of my trips out, I was able to find what appeared to be a museum or library. I was able to slip this tablet into my shirt."

"That's all well and good, but what are their plans for us? They didn't look too friendly," asked Mikja.

"They aren't. As near as I can tell they are a fairly blood thirsty group."

"Why are we still alive?" asked Jake.

"The Borrol have a culture driven by ritual. Their day to day lives are peaceful, but at certain times they have to offer blood sacrifice to appease their gods."

"Like the Rytans on Langor 12," offered Zedra.

"Yes exactly. I'm alive only because it's not time for their yearly sacrifice."

"At least that gives us some time," said Jake.

"Unfortunately not, Mr. Astro, based on what I could gather from their preparations, the sacrifice will happen tomorrow night or the next, at the latest."

"The news keeps getting better. By the way, it's Jake, professor. We need to get out of here and get out of here quick. We have some weapons, but we're not an army. Any idea how many of these things there are?"

"As near as I can tell, there is around a hundred or so total. Although, I have no way of knowing how accurate that estimate is."

Qazjix walked over to the door and started running her hands across the wood and inspecting the condition of the hinges.

"I think Rheylaash and I can break down this door. This ancient wood is weak and the hinges are rusted."

"I agree, but they would be on us before we could get 20 feet. I wish this room had a window so we could see what they're doing. Professor, did you notice where the creatures were when you went out? Was there any kind of regular schedule they would adhere to?"

Professor Naken shook his head.

"No, usually there was only one guard that would come get me and let me walk around. I never saw anyone else the entire time. As near as I could tell, they always stay inside the buildings unless someone wanders in. It was a bit bizarre."

"It also makes it near impossible for us to know when we need to escape. There could be one watching us, or all one hundred. The odds aren't good," said Qazjix.

"These creatures never venture above ground do they?"

"Why yes Jake, that's correct, but how did you know that?"

"It's the eyes and skin. The lack of pigment and enlarged pupils indicate that these are strictly underground dwellers."

"It seems like you might have a plan," said the professor.

"I think I do. We have some ammunition, but not enough to stop the whole group. I do have a limited number of these."

Jake pulled three metal cylinders from his backpack.

"Magnesium flares?" asked Zedra.

"Correct. I brought them in case we needed to signal each other, but they should provide enough light in this small cavern to dissuade the Borrol from following us. From there, we get back up the tunnel and to the hole that we originally came down. We then climb up the rope and we're home free."

"I'm afraid I won't be able to move very fast Jake. I'm not as young as I used to be," said the professor.

"I will carry you professor," offered Rheylaash.

"It won't be my most distinguished moment, but I don't think I have a choice. Thank you Rheylaash."

"When do we go?" asked Mikja.

"They never came to get me during a six hour interval in the night. From roughly 12 until 6, I was always left alone. It's possible that this is some sort of rest period for them."

"It's settled then. We go at 1am. That should give

them time to get settled in and hopefully sleep or whatever they do. I suggest you rest for the next couple of hours until then. Mikja and I are going to go over the plans again."

"I agree Jake, let's rest for the task at hand," said the professor.

"Come Rheylaash and let us meditate," said Qazjix.

"Yes my love. Let us ready our minds."

"Dad, I'd like to get some more questions answered."

"Not now, dear. I want to rest."

"Fine, later then."

The room was filled with silence until the timer on Jake's watch started beeping. Jake hit a button on the side of his watch to stop the beeping and stood up.

"It's time. Remember, we move quickly as I fire the flares. Use your ammunition sparingly; we don't want to get into a fight with these people. They can overwhelm us easily. The key is to keep moving as fast as we can. When we enter the tunnel, beware that damn slime. It'll be tricky, but hopefully it will slow them down as much as us. Rheylaash and Qazjix, are you ready to knock the door down?"

They both nodded. Jake gestured to the door and stepped out of the way. In unison, Rheylaash and Qazjix ran toward the door and struck it with their shoulders. The force of the impact shattered it into a thousand pieces.

"Move quick," said Jake.

Rheylaash grabbed the professor into his arms and took off out the door with the rest close behind. The group had not gotten 30 feet away from the room before the creatures started to pour out of a nearby building. A ringing, that Jake could only assume was a warning bell, started to sound. Jake grabbed the first flare from his bag, pointed it at the ceiling, and pulled the trigger. The bright flare shot to the roof and started to give off a bright light. As Jake thought, even the diminished light hurt the Borrol's eyes and caused them to slow down. Unexpectedly, the flare's light started to ebb soon after it hit the roof.

"Why is the flare dying out so fast?" yelled Mikja.

"It's that damn slime. It's not letting the flare burn like it should. Keep going!"

Rheylaash, Qazjix, and the professor made it to the rocks at the mouth of the tunnel first with Mikja and Zedra close behind. They climbed over the rocks and into the tunnel as the first flare's glow died out. Jake took the second flare out of his backpack and fired it at the roof of the cavern. While Jake scrambled over the rocks, a spear grazed his shoulder.

"Aarrrggghh," moaned Jake as he grabbed his wound.

"Are you ok?"

"Why Zedra, I didn't know you cared," said Jake as he grinned through the pain.

Jake took the third flare from his bag and pulled the trigger. The flare sputtered and failed to launch. Jake threw the useless flare at one of the nearest pursuers, hitting him in the head and knocking him down. As the cylinder fell to the ground, it shot out its flare and struck a second Borrol. The group ran down the tunnel with all but Rheylaash and Qazjix slipping on the slime covered rocks. The Borrol recovered and were soon close behind them. Rheylaash and Qazjix made it to the exit first. After Rheylaash put the professor on Qazjix's back, she started up the rope. As soon as they made it to the top, Zedra started climbing the rope. Jake, Rheylaash, and Mikja crouched beside the tunnel walls and fired down the tunnel, hitting several of the Borrol as they charged.

"I'm out captain!"

"Then get up the rope Mikja."

"Not without you."

"We're right behind you. No one is dying a hero today."

Mikja ran to the rope and climbed, reaching the top of the hole quickly.

"I too am out of ammunition," said Rheylaash.

"I've got one more clip, head for the rope and I'll cover you!" yelled Jake.

Rheylaash reached the rope as Jake fired his last shot. He started to climb as he heard Jake cry out.

"Jake!"

"Go, I can make it."

Rheylaash dropped from the rope and ran over to where Jake had fallen.

"You have a spear in your leg. You will never make it."

Three of the creatures ran toward Rheylaash. He grabbed the closest one and threw him into the other two, knocking down all three.

"This might hurt," said Rheylaash.

Rheylaash broke the spear embedded in Jake's leg off near the tip.

"Aaaaarrrggghhh! A little," said Jake.

Rheylaash threw Jake over his shoulder and ran toward the rope.
He grabbed it and climbed nearly to the surface when one of the Borrol grabbed a spear.

"Behind you!" yelled Jake as the Borrol warrior threw the spear.

Rheylaash held the rope as he pushed Jake up through the hole. The spear missed Jake, but hit Rheylaash in the center of his back. Jake and Qazjix reached back down the hole to try to help pull up Rheylaash who was hanging by his left arm. Another of the Borrol stood and threw his spear. This one struck Rheylaash directly in his chest and caused him to lose his grip on the rope and fall to the ground with a thud. Just as Qazjix moved to jump back down the hole and help Rheylaash, the ground began to shake. Jake pulled Qazjix back as the ground shook harder and harder.

"It's an earthquake," shouted the professor, "we need to get away from here, those tunnels could collapse and kill us all."

Zedra leaned down beside Qazjix as tears streamed down the green goliath's face.

"We need to go. Rheylaash wouldn't want you to die as well. Qazjix! Please!"

Slowly, the grieving giant stood and started running away with the rest of the group. As they climbed out of the valley, they looked back down from where they had come. A large fissure had opened up through the valley that crossed over into a nearby river. Gradually, the valley was filling up with water. The group was viewing the birth of the newest lake on Vega Onias.

"Qazjix, he died saving me and I will always remember that," said Jake.

"Yes, he did."

Qazjix turned and sprinted into the jungle away from the rapidly filling fissure.

"Qazjix!" shouted Jake.

"Let her go, she will need time to mourn. It's their custom to mourn alone, but she'll be ok," said Zedra as she put her hand around Jake's waist.

"Come on Jake, let me help you walk. We're going to need a doctor to look at your leg and shoulder.

Those wounds are a bit too serious for the healing ray."

"Thanks Zedra."

Everyone turned to walk toward town except for the professor who stood looking over the valley.

"Professor? You coming?" asked Jake.

"I am. I just can't help but think about the waste of it all."

With one last look, the professor, turned and started down the trail to town.

Jake spent the next two days resting in bed after getting the town doctor to look at his injured shoulder and leg. While he waited on Jake to get clearance to fly, Mikja was at the ship making final preparations for lift off.

"I hope you're taking care of my ship."

Mikja turned around to see Jake walking toward the ship.

"Good to see you Captain."

"Thanks. Are we about ready to get going?"

"We're ready as soon as you get aboard."

"How's the shoulder and the leg?" asked a voice from behind them. Jake and Mikja turned around.

"It's going to be ok, professor. The doc says no permanent damage."

"Aren't you supposed to be on crutches?" asked Zedra.

Jake ignored the question.

"I've transferred the rest of the money into your account, Jake."

"I appreciate it. It's been nice doing business with you. Are you and your dad going to stay around here for a while?"

The professor shook his head.

"I've been looking at this tablet I was able to save. It's remarkable."

"It's a prehistoric story of a god with unlimited power. The amazing thing is that included in the story is series of coordinates to a planet. This could be the recounting of an ancient alien encounter," added Zedra.

"It does sound intriguing," replied Jake.

"I think it's worth investigating, but I need help. I've got a colleague on Uthoera that can help with a more accurate translation."

"You know by coincidence professor, Mikja and I have some seating available if you'd like to hire us to take you. I can give you a good rate on the trip."

Zedra walked up to Jake and grabbed him by his neck and pinched.

"Owwww. What was that for?"

"So I get a good enough grip to do this."

Zedra pulled Jake close and kissed him. The forcefulness of the kiss surprised Jake, but he wasn't going to complain and he certainly wasn't going anywhere.

"Captain. Captain? It's time to lift off."

"Shut up, Mikja," he said returning to the kiss.

Zedra then pushed away.

"Now what's that rate on the transport?"

"Negotiations are subject to continue."

"Do you have room for one more?" came a weak voice from the hangar entrance.

The group turned and saw Qazjix, head bowed, walking toward the ship.

"The time of mourning is finished and I have nothing keeping me here. I'd like to travel with friends for awhile and not be alone."

"You're always welcome with us."

"Thank you, Professor Naken."

"Load up and we'll get going," said Jake.

Jake pulled a small bag from his pocket and tossed it to Zedra who caught it with a puzzled look on her face.

"What's this?"

"Null gravity sickness pills. I have a feeling that you might need them."

Ashley Sherer

Jake Astro
and the
Pyramid of Death

The
Mystery of the Ancients
Trilogy
Part II

Ashley Sherer

"Activate the null gravity field."

Mikja flipped a green switch on the console and the Obsidian started the slow ascent through the atmosphere.

Jake turned to face the group sitting behind the cockpit.

"If anyone needs null gravity sickness pills, please see Zedra."

"That's not very funny, Jake," said Zedra, her face locked in a tight grimace.

Jake turned his chair around with a small grin on his face.

"Fire up the rockets."

Mikja entered the command into the computer and

white-hot flames shot out of the engines. With a jolt, the ship sped upwards. As the Obsidian rose through the atmosphere, escaping the gravity of Vega Onias, Jake watched out the cockpit window. His mind wandered back to the events of the last few days and he hoped his life could get back to normal.

"Captain? Captain?"

The voice interrupted Jake's thoughts.

"Sorry, what's up?"

"We've exited the atmosphere and are ready to enter the hyperspace curve whenever you're ready."

"Let's do it."

The hyperspace curve drive emitted a low hum as the ship vibrated. As the vibrations increased in intensity, the ship became more and more translucent until it disappeared into the hyperspace curve. Jake unlatched his safety harness and walked to the back of the ship.

"Do we keep the meter running when we get to the spaceport? Or are you done with Mikja and me?"

"You have a very colorful way of talking Jake. I'm afraid you wouldn't be interested in the work we will be doing," replied Professor Naken.

"That's what I figured. Qazjix, you're welcome to come with us."

The Wixilan smiled.

"I appreciate the offer Jake, but Professor Naken has

already offered to train me as an apprentice archeologist. It will be good to get a new start on life."

Qazjix's smile wavered for a split second. Jake couldn't read her mind, but knew that it would be a long time before she would get over the death of Rheylaash.

"Just know that the offer is always good. What about you princess? Wouldn't you like a life of glamor and excitement with Mikja and me?"

Zedra raised her eyebrow at Jake.

"I know, I know. You couldn't bear a to miss what could end up being the find of the century."

"Jake, you know good and well that within 72 hours one of us would be forced out the airlock into deep space."

"They don't want us," yelled Jake to his co-pilot.

"They're not the first," yelled Mikja back.

"We'll be around the spaceport for a few days trying to pick up some work if you need us for anything."

"Thanks Jake. How long will it be till we get to Uthoera?"

"Another hour or so," said Jake as he stood up. "I better go back up front. Just let me know if you need anything."

Jake walked to the cockpit and climbed back into the captain's chair.

"Another day, another dollar, right?"

"This one's different captain. You're going to miss her."

Jake's smile dimmed for a second.

"Maybe, but our life isn't exactly for the academician. She's better off."

"Probably."

Jake shot his co-pilot a dirty look as he settled back watching the bright swirl of the hyperspace curve flash by the viewport. Just as he began to get comfortable, a bright red light started to blink on the control panel.

"Ok guys, we'll be exiting the hyperspace curve in about ten minutes. That puts us on the ground at the Uthoera spaceport in about 30 minutes."

The professor, Zedra, and Qazjix packed up the books that they had been working with.

"I appreciate this opportunity that you both are giving me," said Qazjix to the professor and Zedra.

"It's our pleasure Qazjix. We both believe that you have the temperament and natural aptitude to be an excellent archeologist," Professor Naken replied.

With a slight shudder, the Obsidian exited out of the hyperspace curve and entered into orbit around Uthoera.

"Activate the null gravity field and let's take her into

the spaceport."

As the null gravity field surrounded the ship, the planet's gravity gently pulled them to their destination. The Obsidian's rocket engines fired every few seconds during the descent to make minor course corrections.

"Landing in 30 seconds... 15 seconds... 10 seconds... 5, 4, 3, 2, 1."

The ship shook as it came to rest upon the concrete landing pad at the Uthoera spaceport.

"Lower the ramp and let's get out of here," ordered Jake.

Mikja punched a yellow button on the control panel and the ship decompressed with a loud sustained hiss. As the hiss faded, the ship's ramp lowered to the launch pad.

"Passengers first," said Jake as he unbuckled his harness and stood.

"Always the gentleman," replied Zedra.

After unbuckling their safety harnesses, the professor, Zedra, and Qazjix grabbed their bags and walked down the ramp. Jake and Mikja jogged to catch up with them as a short man dressed in a black suit walked up to the group and extended his hand to the professor.

"Welcome to Uthoera, Professor Naken. Allow me to introduce myself. My name is Petrik Morden. Dr. Kyriakos sent me to bring you and your daughter to the university as soon as you landed. He has made a rather large breakthrough with the tablet."

"Has he finished the translation?" asked the professor.

"No, but he has made significant progress and feels that with you and your daughter assisting, it will be only a matter of time."

"That's wonderful news. However, we do have a slight change of plans," said the professor.

"Change of plans?"

"Yes, allow me to introduce Qazjix. She will be accompanying us."

The green alien stepped forward and extended her hand.

"Hello, I'm very glad to meet you."

Morden ignored her hand and turned back to the professor.

"I'm not sure about this. The Doctor said there would only be two of you."

"There's not a problem is there?" asked Zedra.

"No, no, of course not. Please come this way."

The professor and Qazjix followed Morden as Zedra ran back to Jake. Without speaking a word, she grabbed him behind the neck and pulled him close.

"Goodbye Jake."

She kissed him softly before pulling away.

"Goodbye Zedra."

Zedra ran and caught up with her father, Qazjix and Petrik as they headed to the university as Jake watched them walk away.

"Come on Captain, let's see if we can't find some trouble to get into."

The two men wandered into the spaceport and found the pilot's lounge. Acrid smoke and eclectic music filled the air as humans and aliens from a hundred different worlds milled about inside. Jake sat down at an empty chair at the bar.

"Check out the job board, those credits won't last forever. I'm going to get a drink. Barkeep, one jangu please."

The bartender walked over to Jake and poured a bright green liquid into a small shot glass. Mikja sat down at a computer terminal and started checking out the various jobs posted for those with ships.

"Nothing much here, Captain."

Jake downed his shot and threw a few credits on the bar to pay for his drink. He pushed out his chair and walked over to the terminal. Jake pointed at one entry on the screen as he stared over his co-pilot's shoulder.

"What about that one?"

"Carrying Denobian spice to Argo 14? Don't you remember the last time we were on Argo 14?"

Jake frowned and nodded.

"How was I supposed to know that the governor's daughter was engaged? Ok, fine. What about that one? Transport needed for Rigelan Fire Worms to Marcon Three."

"Have you ever smelled a Rigelan Fire Worm?"

Jake shook his head and walked back over to the bar. After ordering another drink, he turned back to Mikja.

"How about a vacation? I know this one planet where the women are so-"

"Do you remember our last vacation?"

Jake smiled, "No, I can't."

"I can. Let's just see about finding some work and getting off of this world."

"Fine. You continue your quest, I'm going to have another drink."

Five drinks later, Mikja found a job that would agree with both of them.

"Captain, come here and check this out."

Jake stumbled to the terminal where Mikja was seated.

"You're going to need to read this to me, for some reason my eyes just aren't focusing. Must be all the smoke in this bar."

"It wouldn't be the six drinks you've had?"

"Read, before I turn you into luggage."

"You know we were bred.-"

"Read."

Mikja turned back to the screen.

"Ship needed to run electronic parts from Uthoera to Caldera. Must leave today or tomorrow. It pays 5,000 credits with a 1,000 credit bonus if it can be done within two days."

"Done, sign us up. I'm going to have one more."

As Jake walked toward the bar, he bumped into a large red alien with four arms and black curved horns on his head.

"Watch out human scum, you made me spill my drink," the creature yelled, with a low guttural voice.

"Pardon me, sir. I will be happy to buy you another," slurred Jake.

The creature pushed Jake with one of his massive arms and knocked him down.

"Hey, we don't want no trouble in here!" the frightened barman yelled.

Jake stumbled to his feet and swung his fist at the creature's jaw. As the creature ducked, Jake's momentum carried him onto a table where two humans sat.

"Hey, what the-" one of the humans started to say.

One of the men, a large muscular fellow with tattoos and smelling of an open sewer, jumped up out of his chair. He grabbed his beer glass and swung it at Jake's head. As the glass came toward his head, Jake slipped on the beer soaked floor and fell down. The beer glass shattered on the face of the second man who still sat at the table. Stunned for a second, the man at the table grabbed a chair and broke it over his muscular tattooed friend's back. Jake decided that the floor was the safest place in the bar and crawled to the terminal where Mikja still sat.

"The situation appears to have devolved Captain."

"I deem that an accurate assessment. Out the back way?"

"How do you know there's a back way?"

"These places always have one."

Jake and Mikja worked their way through the flying fists and broken glass, until they reached the back door. Just as Jake reached to open the door, it swung open and knocked him backwards into Mikja.

"Hello officer, I believe you are needed in the next room. There is hooliganism afoot," slurred Jake.

The officer nodded as he pulled a control wand from his belt and touched Jake. Fire shot through Jake's body until the room went dark. The officer repeated the process with Mikja. The two men, along with everyone else in the bar, were thrown into holding cells down at the local police station. Jake awoke when a loud clanging echoed through his skull. He rolled over and realized he was lying on a cot.

"Why is there a cot in the bar?" asked Jake.

"Unbelievable. You're gone for six hours and you get a bar shut down and all its customers thrown into jail!"

Jake's head pounded in rhythm with each word shouted out by the angel standing outside the bars.

"Umm, hello Zedra. Could you stop the banging and yelling?"

"No!", *BANG*, "I!", *BANG*, "WON'T!", *BANG*, *BANG*.

"Umm, thanks."

Jake sat up on his cot and swung his legs over to the floor as waves of nausea washed over him. He glanced over to the other cot in the cell where Mikja was sleeping as the old saying went, 'like a baby'. Jake grabbed the bars of the cell and pulled himself up, as the pounding increased in his head.

"Could you please..." Jake ended his sentence and ran over to the toilet where he purged the evil that he had consumed the night before.

Jake wiped his mouth before he staggered back over to the cell door.

"Breath mint?" asked Zedra holding out a white tablet.

"Thanks."

Jake took the mint from her hand and popped it into his mouth.

"Now, can you get Mikja and me out of here? I seem to remember that we've got a job to do."

"Yes, you do, but not the one you had planned on."

Jake sat back down on the bed and held his head in his hands.

"Just what does that mean?"

"It means that my father has need of your services again."

"No deal. I want a nice easy job."

"Those kind of jobs bore you and you know it. Plus they don't offer the chance for wealth beyond belief."

"Wealth beyond belief? That is a well worn cliché."

"Trust me. Are you interested?"

Jake stood up and staggered over to the cell door.

"Are you on the level?"

"I've not lied to you yet."

"Mikja and I will listen to the details, AFTER you get us out of here."

"Done. I'll be right back with the jailor. He should have your paperwork completed by now."

Jake shook his head as he watched Zedra walk out

of the cellblock. Zedra knew his answer before he had even given it, but she was right. The prospect of spending more time with her, beat a shipment of electronics any day. Jake leaned over to the cot where Mikja was stretched out and nudged his slumbering co-pilot.

"I'm not asleep, Jacob Artemis Astro."

"I'm in trouble aren't I?"

The use of Jake's middle name indicated that he had pushed things a little too far with the bar brawl.

"One drink is ok, two drinks are ok. You had at least six."

"Probably a lot more than that. As I crawled on the floor, I found a bottle that rolled off a table. It was still about a third full."

Jake decided to change the subject before he made himself sound even more pathetic than he already had.

"Did you hear Zedra? All that money would be nice. It'd keep you in live mice and birds for a long, long time."

"I heard, and yes it would be nice. Although I wonder if she could offer stale bread and dirty water and you'd take it so you could spend more time with her."

Jake turned to Mikja.

"Don't forget, I'm the Captain and I'll take whatever jobs I want. Understand?"

"Yes Captain."

Before Jake could say anything else, the door to the cellblock opened. Zedra and a uniformed man walked into the cellblock to Jake's cell. The uniformed man took a card from his pocket and inserted it into a slot located to the left of the cell door. As he removed the card, the door slid open.

"Come on Mikja, we've gotten our ticket punched."

Mikja and Jake followed Zedra and the uniformed man out of the cellblock. After signing paperwork and receiving a brief lecture on the value of knowing what a person's limit is when drinking, Zedra, Jake, and Mikja exited the police building.

"Thanks for springing us, but what's the story? You mentioned wealth beyond belief."

"Yes, you've even piqued my curiosity," added Mikja.

"Well I don't exactly have the money right now. But-"

"Come on, let's leave her now. We don't work on credit," said Jake.

Jake and Mikja reversed direction and started back toward the spaceport.

"Wait, wait," Zedra ran after the two men.

"Let me explain. This tablet that my father is trying to translate contains the description of a planet. Located on this planet are magnificent treasures and some sort of special artifact."

"I see problems with that right away. How does a tablet found on Uthoera contain information about another planet? Anybody carving into stone isn't going to be traveling around the galaxy."

"That's a reasonable objection, but if you read the translation, somehow these people provided a star map with the location of eight stars. If you draw intersecting lines between them, there is the planet in the center. Now I know it's crazy, but they've actually been able to verify six of the eight stars."

"You've got my attention, assuming you're right. What's so special about this 'artifact'?" asked Jake.

"No one knows. It's only talked about as the 'artifact'. No mention of what it is can be found, only the incredible power that it possesses. Interested?"

Jake looked at Mikja who shrugged.

"Ok, we're in. What do you need us to do?" asked Jake.

"My father and his colleague Dr. Kyriakos are very close to identifying the last two stars. When they do, we'll need someone to take us there. After we find the treasure, you would get 10% of anything we find."

"20%"

"15% and no more."

Jake looked back at Mikja and both nodded in ascent.

"15% when we find the treasure. Agreed."

"Come on, let's go find dad and Qazjix. We'll get more details from him."

Zedra flagged down an anti-grav taxi and the three took the quick trip to the astronomy building on the university campus. They walked into the white marble building and down a short corridor to an office whose door read 'Emil Kyriakos, PhD. Directory of Astronomy'. Zedra knocked on the door.

"Come in, please," came the voice from the office.

Zedra opened the door and all three walked in. In the room, Professor Naken and Qazjix were seated behind a large brown wooden desk covered with papers. As they peered over the information, a tall muscular man with jet-black hair and olive skin used a magnifying glass to further examine the tablet.

"Doctor Kyriakos, this is Jake Astro, pilot of the Obsidian and his co-pilot and business partner Mikja."

"I'm very glad to meet the both you and I hope that you can be of service to us very soon."

"Does this mean that you and dad have made a breakthrough?"

"Indeed it does. I won't bore you with all the details, but we believe that the intersection of these eight stars point to the fourth planet in the Zarta system. It's an M class world called Otrillon."

"A planet is a very big place to search, Doctor," said Jake.

"You are correct Captain Astro, but we are also fortunate that the tablet contains more than just a star chart. It also details a series of stars that we can use as a guide once we get to the planet."

"Seems reasonable, when do we leave?" asked Jake.

"Jake, that depends largely on you. Can you gather supplies for five people going on a two-week expedition? Here's a list of items I think we will need."

"This shouldn't be a problem, professor, but who's not going?"

"I'm not a field researcher, Captain Astro, so I'll stay here and continue to examine the tablet. You can send be regular reports via subspace radio," answered Kyriakos.

"Mikja and I will get going on this list. It'll take us a few days to get everything we need."

Jake and Mikja left the office as the others continued working with the tablet. While Jake and Mikja acquired the supplies needed, the others re-checked the translation of the tablet and secured the needed permits for the trip. The morning of the trip, the Obsidian had been packed with food, medical kits, weapons, and camping equipment. In addition, a small six-person all-terrain rover was loaded into the cargo hold. Jake and Mikja had just finished loading the Obsidian when Professor Naken, Zedra, and Qazjix arrived at the hangar.

"Good morning everyone, if you'll stow your personal gear and strap in we'll get going."

"It looks like a great day to make a discovery, Jake."

"I agree professor," said Jake as the professor placed his bags in the holding compartment above his seat.

"Good morning, Jake."

"Morning Zedra, Qazjix," said Jake with a nod to each woman.

Zedra and Qazjix strapped into their chairs and within a few minutes, the ship had attained orbit around Uthoera. Mikja punched in the coordinates of Otrillon and the ship entered the hyperspace curve. After only five hours, the ship entered into orbit around Otrillon.

"We're here," Jake announced.

"Do you have the coordinates indicated by the tablet, Jake?"

"Yep, they're on a small island in the southern hemisphere of the planet. We should be over it and ready to land within 20 minutes. One thing, I can set us down on the coordinates, but how do we know what we're looking for?"

"The tablet indicates that the temple is located in the middle of a large plain."

"That seems much too easy. How do we know that this temple hasn't been found and looted?"

"To be honest, we don't know. It's the age-old curse of archeology. We're always in a race with looters and robbers. There may be nothing left."

"Zedra, you didn't mention that possibility when you promised, how did you put it, 'wealth beyond belief'."

"Didn't I? I'm sorry, I could have swore I did."

Jake started to respond when a red light flashed on the console of the ship.

"We're over the island and starting our descent. Everybody buckle up, we'll be on the ground in 10 minutes."

The ship floated like a feather down through the atmosphere using the rocket engines to steer to the coordinates indicated by the tablet.

"Well professor, I don't see any temple and for the record there's not much of a plain. There is a pretty huge forest. Come up here and see what you think."

The professor unbuckled from his seat and went up to the cockpit.

"This actually might be a tremendous break. If the temple is down there, the forest may have hid it from looters. Do you see anywhere that we can land?"

"I see a small clearing south of the site that will be good. We'll have about a five mile hike."

"What about using the rover?" asked Zedra.

"It may be different when we get down on the ground, but that growth looks too thick. I'm afraid we'll have to hike in. Better head back and buckle in, we're landing in about 60 seconds," answered Jake.

The professor walked back to the passenger area and sat down into his seat. The Obsidian floated down through the atmosphere and landed in the middle of the clearing that had been spotted from the air. After lowering the ramp, the group walked out to survey the area around where they landed.

"Excellent job, Captain Astro."

"Thanks, Professor Naken. I'd like to think I'm good at something. Qazjix, can you and Zedra unload the gear?"

"I would be happy to Jake," said Qazjix.

"Sure flyboy," echoed Zedra with a smile.

The large muscular green Wixilan and Zedra went into the ship and began unloading the gear they had brought. While waiting, Professor Naken went over the tablet again to verify the coordinates.

"Jake, I've programmed the positioning device with the location of the temple. It shows that we've got about a six mile hike ahead of us."

"We should get going then, there's no telling how the terrain will be."

The group started off into the forest with Professor Naken leading the way.

"So Zedra, think we can work out some other method of payment if there's no treasure?"

"Hmm, let me think..."

Zedra threw a right cross that knocked Jake to the ground.

"Come on Captain," said Mikja as he extended his hand.

"You know," said Jake rubbing his jaw, "I think if I live to be a hundred, I will never understand women."

Jake took Mikja's hand and stood up.

"Don't feel too bad. This one seems extra difficult. Come on, we better catch up with everybody," said Mikja.

For the next several hours, the party hiked deeper into the lush forest. The dense green foliage slowed their progress to a crawl. Their route took them down through a small valley and crossed over a slow running creek. Once past the shallow water, they climbed up a small hill.

"Guys, I think we're here," said Jake.

The view from the top of the hill revealed a large stone temple. It was about thirty feet high and covered top to bottom in thick, green vines.

"We should split up into two groups and survey the temple. There must be a way in," said Jake.

"Excellent suggestion. Qazjix, Zedra and myself will take the right side."

"I guess that leaves you and me Captain to go left," said Mikja.

Jake nodded. "Let's see what we can find. Everybody stay in contact and don't take any chances."

Jake and Mikja followed the stone blocks around the temple for nearly 50 feet, hacking their way through the thick underbrush. Climbing over a fallen tree, Jake tripped and fell to the ground, scratching his head against something sharp.

"Owwww!"

"You ok Captain?"

"Yeah, I just... wait a second."

"What is it?"

"It's some sort of a flat rock laid down beside the pyramid. Help me clear this off."

The two men cleared off the trees and brush to reveal a large thick slab of stone. In the middle of the stone was a large iron ring.

"Professor Naken, you need to come over here and see this!" yelled Jake.

The Professor, Zedra, and Qazjix hurried around to where Jake and Mikja were inspecting the large iron ring.

"I guess this is the front door."

"I would guess so Jake. The question is how do we lift it?" asked Zedra.

"Could we bring the ship over here and drop some

sort of chain to lift it?" asked Qazjix.

"Or maybe we should blow the door? We do have some explosives," added Mikja.

"Or maybe we don't touch it," said Jake.

Everyone looked at him with surprise.

"Doesn't it strike anyone else a little bit odd that this supposed temple with unimaginable treasure has essentially a big sign that says 'Enter here'. You couldn't ask for a more obvious way of going in."

"I see what you are saying Jake. This is a subtle, sophisticated honey pot," said Professor Naken nodding his head.

"Professor, what is a honey pot?" asked Qazjix.

"Something used to attract someone's attention. In this case, whoever set this one up is trying to distract us from another way in."

The professor bent down and looked closer at the rock.

"I think you're correct Jake. We need to look further, but not on this side. Call it a hunch, but let's search the opposite side and see what we can find. Spread out, go slow and be very observant."

As they walked around the temple, the group hacked and pulled away the vines and small trees that had grown up along the walls. While Jake cleared a small part along the corner of the structure, he pulled a branch away from part of the wall and revealed a small hole.

"Professor! Can you come look at this?"

Everyone rushed over to where Jake stood.

"What do you think about this hole? It's a perfect circle."

Professor Naken took out his flashlight and shined the beam into the hole. He used his free hand and reached in and pulled out handfuls of dirt and vegetation that had lodged in the hole over time. As he shined the beam again into the now clean hole, he turned to Qazjix.

"Hand me the pry bar we brought, please."

Qazjix took the bar out of her bag and handed it to the professor.

"There's a slot at the end of the hole. Your keyhole theory could be correct. I'm going to try to fit the pry bar into the slot and turn it."

Professor Naken inserted the pry bar into the hole and rotated it until the flat edge fitted into the slot.

"Ugghh, I don't think I can turn it."

"Professor, perhaps I would be the logical one to try," offered Qazjix.

"Absolutely," he replied.

The professor stood aside as Qazjix grabbed the bar with her massive hands. As she strained her taut green muscles, the bar rotated a few degrees. Qazjix let go of the bar and rubbed her hands in the dirt.

Once more, she grabbed the bar and for a minute, nothing happened. But then, the bar rotated a little more, and then a little more. With one last effort, the bar rotated a full half turn. A deafening groan emanated from the temple and a cloud of dust flew up from the wall. A section of the wall slid back and created an opening about six feet wide into the side of the temple.

"Wonderful job, my dear."

Jake leaned over to Mikja.

"Remind me not to ever make her mad at me."

"Has anyone who has known you for any length of time not been mad at you?" asked Mikja.

"Good point," responded Jake.

"Dad, would you like to do the honors and lead us into the temple?"

"Thank you dear, but we should all share in the honor. Everyone get out their flashlights and let's see what we can find. Take it very slow and watch out. There could be traps."

The five crept through the dark dusty temple entrance. A long stone corridor led into a large open room with an eight-foot ceiling in the center of the temple.

"This is it? It seems a little anti-climactic. No treasure, no artifact, nothing," said Mikja.

"I don't understand it. This is obviously the temple, unless we're too late and it's been plundered," said the professor as his shoulders slumped down.

"Professor, maybe we should examine the room. There could be a hidden chamber."

"I suppose, Qazjix. Everybody check the walls and the floors, but be careful."

The five spread out shining their lights around the floors and around the walls.

"I think that we may have hit a dry well, professor," said Jake.

"I'm afraid you may be correct. It's so very disappointing."

"If there were thieves, they've stolen everything but the scratches on the wall," said Mikja,

"Scratches?" asked Zedra.

"Mikja, show me the scratches," added the professor.

"Right over here."

The professor and Zedra hurried over to examine the spot where Mikja was shining his light.

"There's not much to see, just a few scratches."

"Do you have some water, Qazjix?" asked Professor Naken.

"I do."

Qazjix pulled a bottle of water from her backpack and opened it.

The professor took the bottle and splashed it over the wall. As the water washed away the dust that had accumulated over the centuries, the scratches began to take form until they resembled the writing on the tablet.

"Well professor, is this a message from the tomb robbers or maybe a description of the treasure?"

"Neither Jake, this is the treasure."

The group gathered closer around the markings on the wall.

"I can't make it out exactly, but this is a map just like the tablet. These are star references here," said Professor Naken as he pointed at the various markings on the wall.

"The ancients didn't make it easy did they?" said Jake.

"No, they didn't. I'm going to start taking pictures of this writing. Please spread out and check the other walls, floor and ceiling for any other writing."

The members of the party scanned each surface within the room. After about two hours of inspection, the entire room had been gone over.

"Professor, I can't find anything else. It seems like every other surface in the room is smooth with only normal signs of wear."

"Thank you, Qazjix."

"I agree with her, there's nothing else here," echoed

Jake.

"I'm finished here with the photos and transcriptions. I think we can leave."

As they walked out of the temple, Jake paused and looked back.

"So all this was just to hold a marker to another place?" asked Jake.

"I think so. It underlines the importance of what we're searching for and it exposes many more questions," answered Zedra.

"Yeah, like who built this temple and how could the same group that carved the tablet carve the message in the wall?" asked Mikja.

"Professor, we better start back to the ship. If we hurry we can make it out of this forest before nightfall," suggested Jake.

"I agree. Let's pack up our gear and start out."

The group gathered up the gear that they had brought and started back to the ship. When they had arrived at the ship, Jake and Mikja started the preflight check, while the rest of packed up and prepared for leaving.

"Jake, can I use the subspace communicator? I want to send a report to Doctor Kyriakos," asked Professor Naken."

"Absolutely, go right ahead. Tell him we'll be leaving shortly."

The professor sat down at the communications terminal and relayed the new information about the temple findings to Kyriakos.

"That's right Doctor, I'm sending you a data stream of all the photos taken plus my notes."

"Excellent, as soon as the data stream completes I will begin the translation. Any other impressions of the site?" asked Kyriakos.

"Nothing that I've not already included."

"Good luck traveling home and I will see you soon."

The professor ended the transmission and sat back down in his seat.

"We're ready to lift off if everyone else is ready?" asked Jake.

Everyone nodded in ascent.

"Hit the null gravity field Mikja, let's go home."

After going through the normal liftoff procedures, the Obsidian soared through the air heading into orbit. About 15,000 feet above the ground, an alarm blared through the ship as red light flashed rapidly on the control panel.

"Everybody hold on!" Jake yelled back to the group.

"What's wrong?" asked Zedra.

"We've lost one of our rocket engines and our null gravity generator is failing," explained Mikja

"What does that mean?" asked Professor Naken.

"In a nutshell, we fall and then we die, if we can't get it working," Jake responded.

The Obsidian descended through the air toward the ground. As it fell, it picked up speed until it was in complete free fall.

"Jake, now would be a great time to do something about this. Jake? Jake?" pleaded Zedra.

"Manual restart on the engines," ordered Jake ignoring Zedra.

"Restart in 45 seconds," responded Mikja.

"No good, we'll be dead in 30 seconds."

"Captain, what about overloading the null gravity generators followed be a full power burn on our one good engine?" asked Mikja.

"We'll have to time it correctly or we'll be splattered against the inner hull. Get ready to do it on my mark."

"20 seconds till impact."

"15 seconds till impact."

"10 seconds till impact."

"Overload the generator," ordered Jake.

Mikja entered the command into the computer as Jake set the one remaining engine for a full 100% burn.

"Impact in five seconds, brace yourselves!" yelled Jake.

The Obsidian crashed into the forest leaving a trail 200 yards long before coming to a rest along the side on a small hill. Jake tilted his head back and let out a sigh as Mikja's hands shook as he tried to unbuckle his harness.

"Is everyone ok?" asked Jake.

"I'm ok. Zedra? Qazjix? Professor?"

"We're-" Zedra started to say.

"The tablet and notes are safe," said Professor Naken as he interrupted Zedra.

"Jake, we're also alright. What happened?" responded Zedra.

"Apparently, we had a failure of both the null gravity generator and one of our engines."

"How does that happen?" asked Qazjix.

"It doesn't. We checked everything out before we left Uthoera and I did a spot check before we lifted off."

"Well something happened, your ship nearly killed us," complained Zedra.

"My ship saved us from being splattered all over the countryside."

"Please, now is not the time for blame," interrupted Qazjix.

"Everybody check yourself, make sure you've not been injured. Mikja, let's see if we can find out what happened."

The professor, Zedra, and Qazjix unbuckled and checked for injuries while Jake and Mikja inspected the different subsystems of the ship. For several hours, the two men went through system after system inside the ship. After verifying that there were no problems with anything inside, they continued outside.

"Come here Mikja. Take a look at this."

Jake pointed to a series of wires and circuit boards inside a panel near the failed engine.

"This power coupling failed and then the backup system also failed. It was the one point common between the engine and the null gravity generator, but I just had this thing overhauled last year. There's no way it should have failed."

"The chances of both the coupling and its backup failing within minutes are astronomical. You know what I think Captain?"

Jake nodded.

"Buddy, this time somebody really may be out to get us."

"What do we tell the others?"

"Nothing for now. It's just a simple, although unlikely, electronic failure."

Both men went back into the ship and addressed the others. Jake explained the failure, leaving out his suspicions of foul play.

"How do we get home?" asked Zedra.

"Fortunately, that's the easy part. The ship has a beacon that sends out a distress signal in the event of a crash. Help should be arriving here in the next 24 hours. I would suggest we all get comfortable and try to make the best of it."

Jake was right, for within 12 hours, the freighter ship Orion had responded to the Obsidian's call on the radio. The freighter had the parts needed for repair and sent them down via shuttle.

As a service robot was unloading the parts, the representative of the Orion addressed the group. "Captain Argo of the Orion wishes to offer passage to any that would like to come back with us."

"Would anyone like to go back on the Orion? Mikja and I can make the repairs and meet up later."

"I think I can speak for Zedra and Qazjix when I say we'll stay with you and travel home to Uthoera together," said Professor Naken.

As the representative from the Orion blasted off for the freighter, Zedra and Qazjix walked over to Jake.

"There's something you're not telling us," said Zedra speaking for the two.

"No, nothing..."

"You're lying. We're both big girls and can take it.

What aren't you saying?"

"I don't know anything but I have a bad feeling. The chance of this happening was too great."

"But things break all the time on spaceships," said Zedra.

"Yes, but that's why we have backups and redundant systems. They failed also. More than that however, this one system that linked into both the null gravity generator and the engines failed. It's almost like-"

"someone wanted to make sure we didn't make it home," finished Zedra.

"Don't tell your dad, I've got no proof."

"What does Mikja think?" asked Qazjix

Jake looked at both women and shook his head.

"Stupid question, pretend she didn't ask it," said Zedra with a smile.

Jake laughed. "You know us well. Let's just get back to Uthoera and we'll investigate what's going on."

"Sounds good."

Zedra and Qazjix started to walk back up the ramp into the ship.

"Qazjix can you help me fit this panel back in. I need your muscle."

The Wixilan turned and walked back to where Jake

was working with the panel.

"I don't need help with the panel, but I didn't want to say this in front of Zedra. I need a favor from you."

"Anything you need, just say it."

"I knew I could count on you. This may be more serious than what I let on. There was clear evidence of sabotage. Will you watch after Zedra and the professor without them knowing?"

"I will watch over them with my life."

"I knew I could count on you. You better get in the ship before Zedra suspects anything."

The flight back to Uthoera went without incident and the Obsidian soon landed at the spaceport.

"Headed back to the university?" asked Jake.

"Yes, the sooner that Zedra, Qazjix and I can get there the better," replied Professor Naken.

"Good luck. We're going to stay here and get the ship ready to go again as soon as you are ready."

"Excellent, Jake. We'll be in contact."

The professor, Zedra and Qazjix hailed an anti-grav taxi and sped off as Jake and Mikja began their preparations. After a few hours, Jake walked up to Mikja.

"Are you finding anything?" asked Jake.

"Nothing, but I'm not gonna lie to you captain. This

one has me worried."

"Yeah, getting bumped off in a fight or a crash comes with the territory, but this..."

"It's dirty and we both know who we have to look at. No one knew where we were going except for us and Kyriakos," said Mikja.

"But why would a university professor of Astronomy want to have us killed. Hell, if we found something, his name would be attached to it. Professor Naken isn't the type to steal credit."

"Even stealing credit isn't worth killing five people. That is cold blooded."

"Do you think Qazjix can protect Zedra and the professor?" asked Mikja.

"Would you want to cross her?"

"Good point."

Beep. Beep.

"You've got a call Captain," said Mikja.

Jake took out his comm device from his pocket and answered the call.

"Yeah, let me put you on speaker."

Jake pressed a button on the device.

"Can you hear me?" the voice on the speaker was Zedra's.

"Go ahead."

"We've made significant progress with the interpretation from the temple. Can I interest you two boys in another expedition?"

"What do you have in mind?"

"It looks like we're going to Esleon. Ever heard of it?"

"Nope, where is it?" asked Jake.

"It's in the Fergon system."

"That's a binary system. Not much life there."

"And Esleon is a dead world. The average temperature is 140 degrees in the daytime and -40 degrees at night. It's not going to be easy," added MIkja.

"One question," asked Jake, "what are the chances that anything will still be there for us to find? After all, the Fergon system may not be the most popular destination but it's not exactly hidden either."

"Truth is we don't know. It could be nothing, another pointer-"

"Or just a room empty of treasure for a thousand years," said Jake.

"Yes, I can't argue and I wouldn't blame you for wanting to get on with a more normal set of assignments."

"Mikja and I talked it over earlier and we're in it till the end. You can count on us."

"Thank you Jake. You have no idea what this means to my father."

"And you?"

"And me."

"We'll get things ready for a trip to a desert world. When do you want to leave?"

"Two days?"

"We'll see you then."

The next two days were filled with Jake and Mikja acquiring the supplies needed for a trip to the harsh barren world of Esleon. Envirosuits would be needed to survive the harsh temperatures. In addition, Jake would make sure that the group was well armed in case their mysterious enemies decided to make a frontal assault. The morning of the departure Jake met Zedra, Qazjix, and the professor as they arrived at the ship at dawn.

"Morning ladies, professor."

"Good morning Jake, where's your co-pilot?" asked the professor.

"Inside making final preparations. Liftoff will be in 20 minutes. Stow your stuff and get buckled in."

As the three walked inside, Qazjix paused by Jake.

"Has the ship had any unwelcome 'visitors'?"

"No. What about the professor and Zedra?"

"There have not been any additional attempts. I have watched them carefully."

"I know you have. Thank you."

"It was my honor. We better get aboard."

"Yeah, Zedra will think we have a 'thing' going."

"That would not be possible. It would end poorly for you," answered Qazjix with a slight smile as she walked up the ramp into the ship.

Jake thought it would be best if he left the ambiguity in Qazjix's statement and followed her aboard.

Everyone buckled in as Jake and Mikja went through final flight preparations. Jake felt a twinge of uncertainty as he gave Mikja the order to engage the null gravity field and the rocket engines. The last two sleepless days had been spent not only preparing for the mission, but also guarding the ship and going over it inch by inch checking for anything wrong. His fears were allayed as the ship performed perfectly and entered the hyperspace curve without incident. Within three days, the ship arrived in orbit around Esleon. Jake had seen binary systems before, but each time took his breath away. The two fiery orbs were locked together in some sort of eternal combat. Tendrils of plasma leapt back and forth between the two stars in an intergalactic fireworks show.

"Prepare for descent."

"Yes sir."

Mikja entered the command into the ship's computer and the Obsidian began the long controlled voyage to the planet's surface. After a smooth fall for half an hour, the Obsidian landed on a small plateau in the middle of the desert located on the only continent on Esleon.

"According to the wall of the temple, this plateau is our starting point. Those three mountain peaks to the south are our reference point. We are to drive straight toward the center peak where we will find some other marker."

"Some other marker?"

"It wasn't clear, but we will know it when we see it."

"Unless it's been stolen, destroyed, or covered up by thousands of years of sand, dust and dirt," offered Mikja.

"Everybody was thinking it, but you had to be the one to say it," said Jake.

"Mikja is right, but we don't have much of a choice," said Zedra.

Jake unloaded the all-terrain rover from the Obsidian and packed it with the equipment and supplies. After putting on the envirosuits to deal with the intense daytime heat, everyone loaded into the rover. Jake estimated that if they had to go all the way to the mountains, it would take four days at the rover's maximum rate of speed. The terrain was dull and unending. There were no markers, trees, or vegetation of any type, only one hill and then another. At the end of the second day of travel, the group stopped for the night to camp. Professor

Naken, Zedra, and Mikja put up the tents as Jake walked up to Qazjix who was checking out the rover.

"I don't want to freak you out, but-"

"The dust cloud that has been following us for the last day?"

"You noticed it too."

"I didn't want to say anything but I'm afraid there's going to be trouble."

"I agree. That's why I packed a special box of party favors," said Jake as he walked over to the back of the rover where a large gray box was packed. Jake opened the box to reveal five rifles and five handguns.

"Humans have such an interesting way of speaking, but I like the way you think. When do we tell the others?"

"It looks like they've stopped for the night and are keeping just close enough not to lose us, but far enough away that we won't detect them. They want us to find the prize first and then take it from us. We should be safe tonight, but we should tell them tomorrow. Let them get one more good night's sleep. What do you think?"

"I agree, better to be rested and have one more worry free night."

"I'm glad we have you along," said Jake with a grin.

"You'll never know how much I appreciate you taking me in."

The rest of the night, the group slept in tents designed to keep out the subzero temperatures. Despite the looming danger, Jake slept well, although he didn't relish the next day's morning conversation. The next morning, everyone packed up the tents and prepared for the day's travels.

"Can everyone hold up on packing everything away and come over here. Qazjix and I need to talk to you."

"You're not pregnant are you Jake?" asked Mikja.

That remark even made Qazjix crack a smile.

"Not hardly, I always take precautions."

"And technically there has to be two people involved," added Mikja.

"Thank you Mikja for the biology lesson. No, this is actually a bit more serious. I don't want to unnecessarily worry anyone, but for the last two days, we've been followed by someone."

"How do you know that?" asked Zedra.

"A couple of days ago, I noticed a cloud about two miles behind us, but I didn't give it too much thought. Deserts are known to have dust storms, so I figured there was one blowing up. However, the next morning after about an hour's travel, I noticed it again. This time it stayed at a constant distance behind us. When we would stop it wouldn't get any closer and when would get back going, it would start up as well."

"I noticed it as well, and Jake came up to me and asked me about it. It confirmed our fears," added Qazjix.

"What do you and Qazjix propose that we do? Should we abort the investigation and try to get back to the Obsidian?"

"No professor, I don't think that's a viable option. If we head back, we'll run right into whoever is following us. Both Qazjix and I think that we need to continue on. We should be safe until we find whatever is out here because we're doing their dirty work for them."

"But what happens if and when we find it? I don't imagine that they'll want to take our picture and pat us on the back," said Mikja.

"Qazjix, could you get the box?"

She nodded and walked to the back of the rover. Qazjix lifted the box and carried it to the group and sat it down. Jake opened the lid and exposed the contents.

"Weapons? What are we supposed to do with these?"

"We defend ourselves. I know it's not something that you and the professor have had a lot of experience with, but I don't think we have much of a choice. Also, I didn't want to say this because I didn't want to worry you, but Otrillon was no accident either. I found evidence of sabotage."

"I appreciate you letting us know, but Zedra and I aren't unfamiliar with rifles. Her mother and I took her hunting many weekends when she was young.

Zedra, do you remember the hunt on Lakos 2?"

"I do," said Zedra breaking out into a smile, "It was-"

"And what about the safari to the high plains on Talgus 5? It was very exciting. You talked about it for months after we got back," interrupted the professor.

"But we haven't gone in years," said Zedra, her smile fading away and being replaced with an icy glare.

"Why did you quit it? It sounds like you really enjoyed going?" asked Jake.

Zedra's blank stare turned into a practiced frown, "We quit a lot of things when mom died."

The professor put his arm around Zedra who pulled away.

"I didn't mean to open up old wounds," said Jake.

"It's alright. I suggest we continue on our way, but be as vigilant as we can," said Professor Naken.

"I agree professor. Qazjix, if you would, please load the box back into the rover. I think this time however, we put the box on top."

As Qazjix loaded the box back into the rover, the rest of the group climbed in. For most of the day, the cloud continued to follow at a discrete distance.

"Professor, I'm beginning to wonder if there's anything left to find. By this time tomorrow, we'll be at the base of the mountains and the message seemed to indicate that it would be before the mountains."

"Jake, that's always part of archeology. Many times we look and time has worn away what we could find."

"You're a better man than me. I like to actually accomplish things."

Screeggggggggg!

The rover came to an immediate halt, throwing the passengers forward.

"Is everyone ok?" asked Jake.

"What was that?" asked Zedra.

"I have no idea, is anyone hurt?"

"I think we're all ok, just a little shook up," answered the professor.

"Everybody hop out and let's see what happened."

Jake and Mikja got on the ground and inspected the undercarriage of the rover.

"I'll be damned. There's desert everywhere for thousands of miles and we run over a rock. Everybody grab on and let's see if we can move the rover," said Jake

Everyone moved to the stuck rover and grabbed the sides.

"On three. One, two, three."

The group strained and slowly lifted the rover off the rock that it was stuck on.

"How bad is the damage Jake?" asked Qazjix.

"I'm not sure until I can crawl under it. All of you might as well sit down and hang on until I can check things out. Mikja, can you give me a hand?"

"Sure captain."

Zedra took her hand and wiped off the rock before sitting down.

"Dad, you need to look at this."

Professor Naken bent down to examine the stone that Zedra had cleaned off. Carved into the stone were several symbols like the ones found on the tablet and also on the wall of the jungle temple.

"This is unbelievable! Everybody break out the shovels."

Jake and Mikja climbed out from underneath the rover and walked over to the rock.

"Jake, it's what we've been searching for."

"What do you mean?" asked Mikja.

The professor got down on his hands and knees and pointed at the top of the stone.

"These carvings are part of the ancient's language. This rock may prove invaluable."

"Let's get digging," said Jake.

Each person grabbed a shovel and started moving the sand away from the stone. After digging down a few feet, Jake propped on his shovel.

"I thought this was just a rock. How much further down do we have to go?"

The professor knelt down and cleared away some more sand with his hands.

"Everyone, this isn't a rock. It's some kind of structure."

With the professor's discovery, the digging continued and within a few hours it became apparent that the structure was actually a pyramid. Soon, enough of the sand was cleared away to reveal the base of the pyramid. As they continued the excavation, a large square door of stone was uncovered. The archway was carved with pictures of strange creatures and the mysterious language from the tablet

"Well professor, how do you suggest we get in? Use the explosives?"

The professor thought for a moment.

"I think we look for another lock similar to what we found on the temple on Otrillon. I think that the same group has built all of these structures across all three planets?"

"Come on, really?" asked Jake.

"Captain, I've been telling people for years that civilizations across the galaxy share a common history. They all tell a story about mysterious gods that visited from beyond. Sometimes they intervene in the world's development and sometime they're just observers."

"Remind me Mikja, to start listening to your ramblings a little bit closer."

"Jake would you and Mikja keep watch over our friends out there while Zedra, Qazjix and I take a look at this door?"

"Absolutely professor. Just give a holler if you need us."

Jake and Mikja took up a position behind the land rover with their binoculars trained on the group two miles away.

"Can you make out any details?" asked Mikja.

"Not really. I can see two rovers and at least four people but there certainly could be more than that."

Suddenly from behind Jake, a loud scratching sound was heard. Both men turned to see the door to the pyramid sliding back.

"Keep watch while I help out the professor."

"No problem captain."

Turning on their flashlights, the four entered the pyramid.

"This looks very familiar, professor," said Qazjix.

"I agree. You can definitely tell that the same people that built the temple on Otrillon built this pyramid here. Same stonework, same floor plan, same everything."

"And the same central chamber, this time with a prize," said Jake.

All eyes turned toward the center of the room. A stone circular pedestal rose three feet from the floor. On top of the pedestal lay two objects, a tablet and a cylinder whose outside was lined with five rows of ruby red jewels.

"What is your opinion, professor?" asked Qazjix.

"Unbelievable, this cylinder isn't just a relic. It's some kind of technology. Jake, have you ever seen anything like this?"

Jake peered closely at the artifact and shook his head.

"Nope doc, it's got to be thousands of years old, but looks more advanced than anything that I've ever seen. What about the tablet?"

"It's the same language as the others. Let's get the artifact and the tablet out in the sun so that we can take a better look."

The professor took both items off the pedestal and carried them outside. He laid them on a table that had been setup to examine their findings.

"I'm going to keep Mikja company and help watch our new friends while you three examine things a little closer," said Jake.

For the next several hours, the professor, Zedra, and

Qazjix examined and photographed the tablet and the artifact.

"I think I need a break dad, I'm going to see how Jake and Mikja are."

"Excellent idea. A break will do us all good. Let's put these things in their cases and take 15 minutes or so."

As the professor and Qazjix carefully stored the objects, Zedra walked over to Jake to see how things were going.

"Any movement from whoever is out there?" asked Zedra.

"Yep, nothing so far. I think we're ok until we're finished with the excavation."

"We're going to have to fight our way out, aren't we?"

"I'm afraid so, but we're well armed. We can put up a pretty good fight," answered Jake.

Zedra looked out over the desert and saw a cloud start to form on the horizon.

"Jake, they're coming. I'll go get the rifles, while you gather everyone."

"Thanks, and Zedra?"

"Yes?"

"Uh, I just wanted you to know that, uh..."

"Me too. We better get ready."

Mikja pulled the rover into position in front of the entrance to the pyramid, while Qazjix distributed the rifles and handguns.

"We don't have unlimited ammo so keep the rifles on semi-automatic. Pick your shots carefully and watch that they don't try to flank us," Jake ordered.

The dust cloud grew larger until two sand-colored desert rovers came into view. The rovers stopped about 20 yards from the temple. A familiar man wearing all black walked out in front of the group with a megaphone.

"Doctor Kyriakos? What is this?" asked Professor Naken.

"Naken, you're such a small-minded fool. I don't think you realize what we're after. This artifact is the key to power and wealth beyond belief."

"You're the fool, Kyriakos. This artifact could destroy us all," replied the professor.

"Enough talking. Surrender the artifact and we will let you live, resist and you will die."

"We're armed and we will defend ourselves. Back away," yelled Jake.

The two rovers rolled toward the pyramid.

"This is your last chance. Back away," warned Jake.

The rovers continued closer and closer.

"Get ready to fire a warning shot above their heads to

show them we mean business."

Each of the party aimed their rifles angled slightly above the heads of the invaders.

"Safety's off! Please back off!" yelled Jake.

The two rovers continued driving closer.

"Fire!"

Click. Click. Click. Click. Click.

Jake stared at his weapon as the others slowly lowered theirs. The men from the rovers climbed out, never wavering, as they aimed their rifles at Jake and the others.

"Now, those guns can't fire with the firing pins removed. Zedra, be a dear and come bring us the artifact," said Doctor Kyriakos.

Zedra's lips curled into a smile that was more of a snarl as she dropped her rifle and walked over to Kyriakos with the artifact.

"See Jake, things aren't always what they seem."

"You're working with them? But you were almost killed when we left Otrillon," said Jake.

"Very true. After that attempt, I realized that Doctor Kyriakos was the only one that could have been responsible. You see, I had my own plans for the artifact, but I thought it would be more efficient if we joined forces and split the profits. He was most amenable to the idea."

Kyriakos, Zedra, and their men climbed into the rovers.

"I could shoot you, but that would be too quick," said Zedra.

Zedra motioned to several of her men. The men fired their rifles into the group's desert rover.

"This way it will be nice and slow. One hundred and thirty degrees in the day," said Kyriakos.

"140," corrected Zedra.

"That reminds me, everyone take off their envirosuits and toss them in the back of this rover. We don't want to make things too easy do we?" added Kyriakos.

The four did as they were told and when they had finished, the professor looked at Zedra almost in tears.

"Zedra, how can you do this?"

"Let me guess, money and power. Am I right?" asked Jake.

"Oh, more than money and power. I'm going to be known for more than being Professor Naken's daughter."

"Lot's of daddy issues. Great," said Jake.

"Jake, if you were twice as good as you think you are, you'd still only be half the man I'd want."

Zedra turned toward Qazjix.

"I hope you really never thought that an overgrown green freak could ever be a serious scientist."

"You won't get away with this," Qazjix responded.

Zedra ignored the comment and turned toward her father.

"Oh, daddy?"

"Yes, Zedra?" responded the professor as he looked down at the ground, a single tear welling up in the corner of his eye.

"Look at me."

"What?"

The professor raised his head.

Zedra raised her pistol and fired a single round into her father's skull.

"Goodbye."

Zedra sat back down in the front of the rover as she, Kyriakos and the men sped away into the desert.

Jake Astro
and the
End of the World

The
Mystery of the Ancients
Trilogy
Part III

Ashley Sherer

Jake bowed his head as Qazjix placed the wrapped body of Professor Naken into the grave the two had just dug. Drops of sweat made tiny craters in the newly turned sand as Jake and Qazjix filled in the grave. Each shovelful was a grim reminder of the evil act that had taken place just a few hours earlier.

Qazjix turned to Jake as she rested on her shovel. "There is so much evil in Zedra for her to have done this to her own father."

"I never cared much for my father, but even at his worst, I could never do something like this. She fooled all of us, but I'm not going to let her get away with it," replied Jake.

"My mother killed my father in a fit of rage when I was just a girl. It led me away from the way of violence that affects so many of my people. It was the reason I made Reylaash my life mate. He was full of peace and serenity. You will have my help to

121

bring Zedra to justice. This I promise."

The two stood in silence looking at the newly filled grave as Mikja walked up after inspecting the damaged desert rover.

"Captain, I'm sorry to interrupt, but we've got problems."

"You're the master of the understatement," said Jake.

"It's a cliché, but I have good news and bad news. Which one would you like first?"

Jake shrugged. "Good news first."

"I think I can get the rover running. Thankfully, the bullets didn't completely destroy the essential systems. It'll run slow, but it will run."

"How slow are we talking?" asked Jake.

"About half speed at best. We could run day and night, that would get us back in five days."

"That's good news, give us the bad."

"Since they took the envirosuits, we'll be dead before we could get half way to the Obsidian. That is, assuming they haven't destroyed the ship or stolen it."

Qazjix spoke up. "What about rigging up a canopy to keep the heat and sun directly off of us? It might make things a bit more bearable."

"Hmmm, I guess we could use one of the tents and it's poles."

Jake shook his head.

"Still no good. Even if it works we're still as good as dead."

"Why?" asked Qazjix.

"Even if we could keep the heat off of us during the day, we'd freeze at night. Hell, we might freeze tonight. I suggest since it will be dark soon, we set up our tents inside the pyramid and build a fire to help keep us warm. Maybe tomorrow things will look better."

"Even if it doesn't we'll need to make a decision one-way or another," added Mikja.

"I've been thinking about it. We cut up the remaining tent and sleeping bags to make three makeshift envirosuits for the night travel. We'll be cold and miserable, but we should be able to live. I can't order us to do this and I'm certainly open to suggestions," said Jake.

"It sounds like the most logical course of action, Jake."

"I agree with Qazjix, Captain. I'd rather go down fighting than just waiting to die here in this pyramid."

The night in the pyramid was uncomfortable, but livable. The pyramid stone had absorbed some of the intense heat from the day. Thanks to the fire and the warmth from the tents, no one slipped into hypothermia. The next morning, the three sat around the fire and had a small breakfast. Their food would have to be rationed to last the duration of the trip.

"Captain, I'm going to get started with the canopy."

"Ok, Qazjix and I will see if we can't make some new improvised envirosuits."

After breakfast, Mikja started the assembly of the makeshift canopy over the rover. He removed the steel rods from the walls of the tents and secured them to the four corners of the rover using nylon thread unraveled from the tent fabric. Next, he took the remaining tent and cut it into a rectangular shape. He then threaded the edges around the poles attached to the rover. As Mikja worked with the rover, Jake and Qazjix worked on creating three homemade envirosuits for wearing at night. Qazjix used her knife to cut two armholes on the side of the bag. She then cut a flap at the bottom. When the temperature fell, they would be able to slip into the sleeping bags upside down and use the flap to see out of. It would limit their vision, but offer more protection from the cold desert winds.

"Should we take the guns?" asked Qazjix.

"Take the ammo, since we can use the powder if we needed to, but the guns are useless. We also need to strip out as much extra weight from the rover as we can. If we take out the second and third row of seats it will lighten the load significantly. Maybe it'll even give us a little extra speed," said Jake.

"When do we leave?" asked Mikja.

"Unless anyone has any objections, I say we leave as soon as the sun starts going down today. We might as well find out sooner rather than later if our makeshift suits are going to keep us alive."

Both Mikja and Qazjix nodded in agreement. Jake used Qazjix's knife to loosen the screws that held down the second and third row of the bench seats in the rover. When he had them undone, he and Mikja lifted the seats and tossed them out onto the sand. Jake spread the remains of the third tent across the metal frame of the rover. The fabric would help to keep the frame from being too hot or too cold to sit upon. When Mikja and Jake had removed all they could from the rover, Jake walked into the pyramid to tell Qazjix that they would be leaving soon.

"It looks like Zedra took off too soon," said Qazjix.

"Why do you say that?"

"These symbols here on this wall seem to have more information about the artifact. I can't read them yet, but perhaps with the professor's notes I can do the translation."

"I know you can, but you've only got 10 more minutes till we leave. We don't want to push our luck."

"No problem. I'll be done in five minutes."

Jake walked back out to the rover.

"Is our newest little archeologist nearly finished?" asked Mikja.

"Cute. I wouldn't call her that to her face."

"I'm a lizard, not an idiot."

"Those two things are not mutually exclusive, but to answer your question, she'll be out soon. How are we here?"

"Ready as soon as she gets out. Come on let's triple check things."

As Jake and Mikja inspected the rover, Qazjix joined them.

"I'm ready, when the both of you are."

"I think we're done. Let's get aboard and get started."

Jake slipped into the driver's seat as Mikja sat beside him. Qazjix stretched out in the back and reviewed the notes she made from the inside of the pyramid using a small penlight for illumination. For the first couple of hours, they rode in silence, conserving their energy. As the sun descended below the horizon, Jake stopped the rover.

"We need to get into our suits before it gets too cold."

"What's the temperature?" asked Mikja.

"Right now, the gauge says 80 degrees."

"So it's dropped about 60 degrees in an hour?" asked Qazjix.

"Correct. I know both of your species don't function well in the intense cold, so I don't want to take any unnecessary chances."

"These things aren't exactly the most comfortable,"

said Mikja as he pulled his suit up over his shoulders.

"Would you rather be a frozen block of lizard?" replied Jake.

Mikja grunted as he tightened the makeshift suit around him.

"How's your suit, Qazjix?"

"It isn't exactly a perfect fit, but I believe it will protect me sufficiently."

Jake pulled his suit over his head and sat back down in the driver's seat of the rover.

"Ready?"

Both Mikja and Qazjix nodded.

Jake fired the rover up and started back on the journey toward the Obsidian. Periodically, he glanced at his two passengers to check for signs that the cold was bringing their body temperature dangerously low. For the next three hours, the temperature dropped like a stone from 80 degrees when they had put on their suits to -25 degrees according to the onboard thermometer. As predicted, due to their physiology, both Mikja and Qazjix, became sluggish and non-responsive as their body temperature fell. Over the next eight hours, Jake drove on his own, struggling to keep the rover on course, as his hands grew numb and teeth chattered until his jaws ached. One more mile, one more hill, Jake thought to himself until his perseverance was rewarded. A sliver of light broke over the horizon, growing larger until Jake had to squint. Another hour into the trip, the increase in temperature brought life back to Mikja and Qazjix.

"Uhhh, what happened?" asked Mikja.

"Is it morning?" added Qazjix.

"To answer both of your questions, you both fell into hibernation when the temperature dropped and yes it's morning."

"Are you ok, Jake?" asked Qazjix.

"Much better now that the temperature has risen," said Jake with a smile.

"What's the temperature?" asked Mikja.

"A balmy 70 degrees."

"Jake, why don't you stop? We will take turns driving while you get some sleep," suggested Qazjix.

"I won't argue with that."

Jake stopped the rover and hopped out onto the desert sand. His muscles screamed in agony as he stretched to get his blood flowing. He groaned as he removed the makeshift suit that kept him from freezing to death just a few hours earlier.

"You sure you're ok, captain?" asked Mikja.

"Yeah, I didn't move too much last night while driving and now I'm paying for it."

"Take your time. We can wait," said Qazjix.

"Time is the one thing we don't have. We better get going," replied Jake as he climbed into the back of the rover. He rolled up his suit and used it for a pillow as he reclined under the makeshift sunshade.

"I can drive first," offered Qazjix.

"Sounds good to me," said Mikja.

During the day while Mikja and Qazjix swapped out driving, Jake slept a few hours before the temperature made it far too hot to be able to rest.

"Are we there yet, are we there yet, are we there yet?" asked Jake from the back of the rover.

"You know captain, that's not funny when you do it aboard the Obsidian so it's really not funny now that you're doing it here."

"Oh, I don't know. What do you think Qazjix?"

"I find that often you think you are funnier than you truly are."

"Ouch."

The rest of the day continued with the trio mostly in silence, conserving their energy. The water they had brought was rationed out to a few sips a day along with a few meager bites of survival rations.

When the sun started to set, Jake slipped on his suit and took over the driving. Just as on the first night, Mikja and Qazjix slipped into their hibernation comas. It didn't seem possible to Jake, but he thought it was even colder on the second night. Jake took care to stretch his arms and legs as much as the cramped rover would allow. As the long evening hours progressed, Jake's eyelids grew heavier. A few times he had to snap out of going to sleep. After a few more hours, following the rover's compass, Jake smiled as the new day's sun started to creep over the horizon. As the temperature started to rise, just as the day before, Mikja and Qazjix stirred from their sleep. The group had survived to make it to the third day.

"Ready for breakfast, captain?" asked Mikja.

"Absolutely, scrambled eggs, bacon, and some freshly squeezed orange juice, please."

"Of course, here you go," replied Mikja as he passed a small cup and half a survival bar.

"Yum, exactly as requested. Give yourself a raise and you are now my chief butler."

"Why thank you sir."

Qazjix laughed as both men stared.

"Just exactly what is so funny?" asked Jake.

"I am amused that in the face of possible death you two act like young children playing grown-up."

"I would have thought you'd know by now all space pilots are young children," replied Jake.

"Regardless of the species, it's a universal constant," added Mikja with a laugh.

Jake handed the cup back to Mikja who poured out a small amount from a canteen and gave it to

Qazjix. She drank it down and passed it back. After drinking his ration for the day, Mikja screwed the top back onto the canteen and put away the cup.

"In all seriousness, how are we doing on supplies?" said Jake as he slid out of the rover and stretched.

Mikja's smile faded, "That was it boss. The canteen is now dry as a bone and we're out of survival bars."

"I'm not worried about the food so much, but if we don't hit the Obsidian in the next couple of days and get some water we could be in real trouble."

"Get some sleep Jake, we'll take over."

Once again, Jake slipped out of his suit and climbed into the back of the rover under the canopy. Within minutes, Jake had fallen into a deep sleep, not bothered by the ever increasing temperature.

"Captain, time to wake up. Captain?"

The voice stirred Jake and confused him. He had just closed his eyes or so he had thought. As his vision focused, he could see the sun starting to set on the horizon.

"I'm up," Jake grunted.

"You had us worried, Jake," said Mikja.

"Yeah, Captain. We couldn't decide whether to just let you sleep or wake you up."

"I'm glad you let me sleep, I think. Any idea how much longer until we reach the Obsidian?"

"I hope we can reach it by tomorrow, but that's a guess," said Mikja.

"We can hope you are correct."

The third night went by with no incidents, but by morning, Jake noticed his lips which had been chapped, were now cracked and bleeding.

"How's it going Jake?" asked Qazjix.

Jake tried to respond but couldn't seem to make the words form with his mouth.

"Jake, are you ok?"

"What's wrong with the Captain?"

Jake eyes had glazed over and without warning he fell onto the steering wheel. The rover jerked to the right and headed toward a large sand dune.

"Grab the wheel and I'll move him," yelled Mikja as he pulled Jake to the side of the rover as Qazjix grabbed the wheel and got the rover back on track. She then climbed over to the front seat and managed to bring the rover to a halt.

"How is he?" she asked.

"Not good. He's stopped sweating. I'm going to get him under the canopy," said Mikja.

"Do you need help?"

"No, I need about a gallon of water, but since that's not going to happen, just keep going."

Qazjix continued on course while Mikja tried to make Jake comfortable. They continued for the rest of the day until the sun started to set.

"What do you think?" asked Qazjix.

"I think we should have hit the Obsidian by now."

"I'm not so sure."

"Why do you say that?"

"Based on our average speed, I think we're still another day away from the ship."

"This is one time I'm hoping that you aren't correct with your calculations. The captain can't last much longer. Let's go as far as we can and then we'll huddle up back here and wait out the night."

Qazjix drove for another hour before she stopped the rover.

"Everything ok?" asked Mikja.

"It's getting too cold. I feel sluggish. How are you and Jake?"

"He seems to be stable, but we need to get him water quick. I'm feeling the cold as well. Let's stop for the night and hope we find the ship tomorrow."

"I agree," replied Qazjix, as she stopped the rover and climbed into the back with Jake and Mikja. The three huddled together as they waited for daybreak.

The next morning as the sun rose over the horizon, Qazjix awoke and checked on Jake. While his breathing was shallow and his skin was pale, he was still alive. Within a few minutes, Mikja woke up as well.

"I'll drive if you want to watch the captain," said Mikja.

"I will."

Mikja got into the front of the rover and continued the long slog through the desert. As Qazjix had predicted, on the sixth day the rover came over a hill and from a distance, Mikja was able to see the Obsidian. Just as night fell, the rover had finally made it to the ship. Mikja climbed out of the rover and crawled into the Obsidian. He gathered up three bottles of water and as he drank one he took the other two out to the rover. Qazjix took her bottle and drank it down, but Jake was non-responsive. Mikja took the bottle and poured it down Jake's throat and over his face.

"Is he going to be ok?" asked Qazjix.

Jake coughed and spit up some of the water.

"Are you trying to kill me? I swear I will make you into a nice pair of shoes."

"I think he'll be ok. Let's get him in the ship. Humans are not quite as hardy as we are. They need a bit more water. Poor engineering, you know," said Mikja.

Mikja and Qazjix each put a shoulder under Jake's arms and carried him into the ship. They laid him down in one of the passenger chairs and gave him more water. After drinking about half a gallon,

Jake's mind began to clear from the heat induced haze he was in. After another half gallon, Jake tried to sit up, but the ache in his head convinced him to lie back down for a few more minutes.

"You had us worried for a second, Captain."

"I had me worried. How are you and Qazjix?"

"We are going to be fine Jake. Wixilan and Lacertilians aren't as water dependent as humans are," said Qazjix as she sat down beside him.

"I was thinking Captain, even though it doesn't look like Zedra did anything to our ship we might want to inspect it before we take off."

"I agree, but let's get some rest tonight. We'll inspect the ship tomorrow morning at dawn."

Early the next morning, after getting the first good night's sleep in a week, all three reluctantly crawled out of their bunks and started inspecting the Obsidian. For the next several hours, the ship was scrutinized from one end to another both inside and out. Every panel and hose was carefully looked over. Exhausted with their effort the three sat down on the entrance ramp of the ship.

"This is a bit odd, I don't see where they've done anything," said Qazjix

"Neither do I and it worries me," responded Jake.

"Captain, do you suppose that they were in such a hurry that they didn't do anything?"

"I suppose it's possible. Did you run a full diagnostic

on the computer?"

"I did, and it shows that everything is just as clean as it can be."

"My guess is that they know that even if we lived, they can beat us to the planet and then nothing else matters. After all, the legend portrayed this weapon as something so fearsome that the ancients wouldn't even describe it. How's the translation coming Qazjix?"

"I've made significant progress with the translation. This cylinder is the key to a device that releases tremendous energy. The ancients theorized that there are many dimensions coexisting side by side. These dimensions are kept separate by an immensely powerful energy wall. Think of it like the walls of a microscopic cell. They calculated that this energy was so powerful that tapping into it for a few milliseconds could power a planet for years. They planned to create a series of devices to tap into the energy. All total there were 12 devices created."

"That sounds like a dream. Why then hide the device and the key?"

"Apparently, when they attempted to breach the dimensional walls, enough energy flooded our dimension to destroy the planet that contained the device. The idea of unlimited energy proved to be too alluring, so they kept repeating the process, planet after planet. After atomizing 11 separate planets, with two billion lives lost, the aliens decided that they couldn't continue their experiments. They were too prideful to destroy the last device because they assumed that they would be able to solve the problem of the massive energy release. To make sure that the device would not be accidentally activated again they separated the device and the key. The hope was that in the future, when their technology had advanced sufficiently, they would be able to activate the 12th device. Unfortunately, their civilization went into rapid decline for some unknown reason before it finally collapsed. All that we have left are these legends that have been passed down."

Jake shook his head.

"If I know Zedra, she's thinking that this device can be sold on the black market. Do we know where they are now?" asked Jake.

"I'm not as good as the professor, but I think I know where they're heading. I've identified the eight stars used as reference. It's a sector of space in the gaseous nebula, Galus 4. The problem is that there's nothing there. No planets on the charts. Maybe I've made a mistake?"

"No I'll bet you haven't. You can hide a lot in a nebula. We've taken refuge in them from time to time when our cargo was, shall we say, less than legal."

"Imagine how much money could be made if you could destroy a planet," said Mikja.

"Imagine the type of organization that would want to destroy a planet," added Jake.

"It sounds like we're in agreement that we're going," said Qazjix.

"So three against at least eight? Is that smart? Plus we don't exactly have any weapons."

"We've got a few weapons on board, plus if this thing is as dangerous as the tablets indicate, we really don't have a choice. What do you think Qazjix?"

"I vote we go now. I am ready to meet Zedra again. I have business with her."

"Mikja?"

"Who wants to live forever? Let's do it."

"Good, set course to the coordinates Qazjix supplied and let's get on the way."

Within a few minutes, the Obsidian began the long ascent into space. Once it attained orbit, Mikja entered the command to enter the hyperspace curve and the ship was on its way. After a two day voyage, the Obsidian arrived at the nebula. Testifying to her accurate analysis and translation of the alien language, the planet was exactly where Qazjix had specified. Mikja scanned the surface, as the planet rotated beneath the Obsidian, a blip appeared on the screen.

"Captain, I've got something."

Jake peered over the shoulder of his co-pilot.

"I've picked up a spaceship. It's located on a plain on the main continent of the planet. We got lucky that this is such a small world. In addition, there appears to be some sort of structure near the ship."

"Do they know that we're here?" asked Qazjix.

"It's possible, but they've not shown any interest if

they do. They're not in a warship so they best they could do it ram us, which would not do them any good as well."

"What are they in?" asked Jake.

"It looks like a class four transport ship. Big enough to hold a couple of dozen men and equipment, if they wanted."

"So they figure to take any intruders out after they land?"

"That's my best guess," answered Mikja.

"Are you getting any energy readings from the ship or the structure?"

"Nothing Captain, which is a little bit odd. You'd think that we'd pick up something from the ship at least, but we're not getting anything. Could their ship be emanating some sort of dampening field?"

"It's possible, or it could be emanating from the structure itself."

"Jake, I think we have to risk it."

"Why don't we come in on the opposite side of the temple?" asked Mikja.

"We could but it looks like there's only one entrance, we're going to have to go around anyway."

"Then let's just go through the front door. Set the Obsidian down behind their ship," said Jake.

Mikja entered the command into the navigation

computer and the Obsidian descended down to the planet's surface. As the ship grew closer to the ground, the features of the temple came into focus. It was a large gray stone building with ornate columns and spires that went around the entire perimeter. A large set of open double doors appeared to be the only entrance into the building.

"Scan the temple again," ordered Jake.

"Nothing."

"What do you mean nothing?"

"I mean that it registers as a shape on the sensors, but that's it. The scanners detect no energy, no temperature hot spots, absolutely nothing. I can only say that it's a structure consisting of something that looks like stone. It's just about a perfect circle with a radius of approximately 300 feet. It might have 2 floors, but that's just an assumption based on the height of 25 feet."

"We should be getting more than that this close even if there is a dampening field."

"I agree, but it's nothing. Still want to set down?" asked Mikja.

"Yep, too late to turn back now."

Mikja landed the ship 20 yards behind Zedra's ship.

"Grab the rifles and the scanners. I'll get my pistol," said Jake who opened a compartment beside his seat and pulled out a grey steel pistol.

"Will do," replied Mikja as he unbuckled and went to

the supply locker.

Jake and Qazjix unbuckled from their seats and gathered at the back of the ship. They were joined by Mikja carrying three semi-automatic rifles, ammunition, and a black handheld scanner. Mike gave Jake and Qazjix a rifle and several clips of ammunition each.

"I've never seen this type of scanner before," remarked Qazjix.

"It's a fairly old model, but still reliable-"

"Until they short out," finished Mikja.

Qazjix chuckled as Jake continued, "-as the newer models. They don't have all the bells and whistles of the newer models, but in terms of infrared, density analysis and temperature operations, they do fine."

"Are we ready?" asked Jake.

Both Mikja and Qazjix nodded.

"Everybody keep their eyes and ears open. I'll take point," said Jake as he pushed the button to lower the ramp.

Jake started down the ramp with his rifle in hand, Mikja and Qazjix behind him, both of them carrying rifles as well.

"Now that we're down on the ground, have your scanner readings changed?" asked Qazjix.

"Nothing, even if there is a dampening field, I should be able to pick up the field itself. Stay out here, I'm going to check out the ship."

Just as Jake stepped out from the Obsidian, two armed men swung out from Zedra's ship and fired several times toward him. Rifle bullets clanged against the armor plating of the Obsidian. Jake quickly ducked back up into the ship as Mikja and Qazjix gathered near the exit.

"They know we're here."

"Masterful understatement, Captain. What's the plan?"

"They've got us pinned in here pretty good, however I don't think they know about the access port in the front of our ship. I think that while two of us draw their fire, one of us could sneak out that port and flank them from behind."

Qazjix stepped up beside Jake.

"Jake, I will volunteer. I can stop them."

"Are you sure Qazjix?"

"Do you doubt my ability?"

Jake shook his head and led Qazjix to the front of the ship to the port. Qazjix slipped out of as Jake returned to the back of the ship where Mikja was. Both fired in an attempt to distract the two men from Qazjix's approach. The firefight went on for a few more minutes before Jake and Mikja's shots were met with silence.

"All clear, Jake," came Qazjix's voice.

Jake and Mikja hurried from the Obsidian over to the other craft. Qazjix was standing over the bodies of the two men who surprisingly didn't seem to have any bullet wounds.

"What did you do to them?"

"The human neck is extremely fragile. It was a simple matter to slip behind them and disable them."

"But didn't the other guard notice when you grabbed the first one?"

"I was fortunate that they were close together. I was able to grab one guard's neck in one hand and the other guard's neck with my other hand."

"You broke their necks with one hand?" asked Mikja, his mouth agape.

"As I said, the human neck is extremely fragile."

Jake made a mental note to never ever get Qazjix mad at him.

The three climbed up the gray stone stairs leading to the open double doors. Inside was an empty expansive ornate entrance hall that stretched for 20 yards. Dust covered every inch of the room except for a large group of footprints on the floor. There were two sets of intricately carved white marble columns holding up large stone archways. Qazjix walked up to the column nearest to the group.

"These markings are very similar to the ones we have encountered so far. I wish I had time to translate them."

"Perhaps on the way out," replied Mikja.

"Come on. Let's keep going," added Jake.

Jake started in with Mikja and Qazjix following behind. After walking a few feet inside the room, Jake turned back to talk to the other two.

"We don't have any idea what the layout is of the inside of this place. With all the columns, there could be people hiding anywhere. Be careful. Mikja, you take the right, Qazjix you take the left and I'll go up the middle."

As the three walked through the room, they continued to see familiar looking designs and markings similar to what that had been seen on Esleon and Otrillon. Out of the corner of Jake's eye, a shadow appeared near the front of the room.

"Take cover!" yelled Jake.

A cloaked figure swung out from behind a column at the end of the room with a rifle pointed at them. As bullets sprayed all around the trio, Jake fell to the ground and rolled behind a column. He breathed a sigh of relief as he saw Mikja and Qazjix both safely behind cover. As she crouched behind one of the columns, Qazjix leaned out and fired her rifle, the shot narrowly missing the dark figure.

Thmmmmp.

The sound of a bullet ripping through flesh came from the opposite side of the room. Jake looked over to see Mikja drop his rifle and grab his leg. As blood spurted from his wound, Mikja slumped down to the floor.

"Cover me, I'm going to check on Mikja!"

Qazjix nodded and fired several bursts as Jake crawled across the floor to the opposite side of the room by Mikja.

"Always looking for attention aren't you?"

"Absolutely, Captain."

"How bad is it?"

"Not good. The bullet went completely through. I'll live if I can get this blood loss stopped."

Jake tore a strip off the bottom of his shirt. He wrapped it around Mikja's leg and tied it off above the bullet wound. The blood loss slowed, but didn't totally stop.

"You need to get back to the ship. The med kit can close that up. Can you walk?"

"Help me up and let's see."

Jake put his arm around Mikja and lifted him to his feet. The lizard man grimaced and sat back against the column.

"Hold on."

Jake leaned out and fired his rifle at the gunman in the front of the room. The bullet struck him in the head and his body fell to the floor. Before any reinforcements could arrive, Qazjix sprinted across the room to join Jake and Mikja.

"You couldn't have done that before I got shot?" quipped Mikja.

"The captain has a flair for the unnecessary," added Qazjix.

"I can't let you two have all the fun. Now let's get Mikja back to the ship."

Mikja shook his head and pulled himself up.

"No. I can get back there. This tourniquet should hold until I get to the med kit. You two need to stop Zedra."

Jake looked at his co-pilot and nodded.

"We'll take care of it, you just get that bleeding stopped."

"Good luck."

"Thanks Qazjix. Remember, if things weren't tough enough with this field or whatever it is, the communicators will be useless. You'll be on your own."

"The news gets better and better," said Jake with a grin.

"Ok, now that I've made you happy, you two get going."

Mikja turned and limped out of the room, using his rifle as a crutch, as blood dripped down his leg onto the floor. Jake and Qazjix started toward the exit on the far side of the room, stopping to check out the lifeless gunman.

"Party favors," said Jake with a smile on his face.

"Party what?"

Jake held up three small gray metallic spheres.

"He's got stun grenades. They use a special light frequency to temporarily disorient anyone looking at them. When I throw one, be sure to look away for a few seconds."

"I will be sure to do that. We're lucky he didn't use them on us."

"Yep, are you ready to continue?"

Qazjix nodded.

Jake peered around the corner to the left and then back to the right. To the left, a stone block wall blocked their path. To the right was a long curved stone corridor. There were no signs of any more of Zedra's men.

"It appears that this is a one way maze," observed Qazjix.

"One way in, one way to die."

"Nice thought."

Jake and Qazjix crept along the inner edge of the wall and made their way down the corridor. Unlike the decorative designs and pictures that had covered the entrance hall, the corridor walls were completely barren. Like the outer room, however, everything was covered in dust and a musty smell permeated everywhere. After they walked another 40 yards, they came to a doorway to another room.

"What do we do if someone pops out from that entranceway?" asked Qazjix.

"We hope that we are a better shot than they are."

Jake got down on one knee and peered into the room. Like the entrance hall, there were two rows of elaborately carved columns along each side. Jake motioned to Qazjix and the two of them crept into the chamber, alert for any danger present.

"Jake, look!" said Qazjix pointing at one of the columns.

Jake gasped as he saw a body on the floor surrounded by a dark red pool of blood. The two walked over to examine the body. The source of the blood was obvious; a sharp stake had pierced the body through the heart. The source of the stake was also obvious as Jake and Qazjix approached the body. Jake saw a hole in the nearby column approximately chest high.

"This makes our job more difficult, if there are traps," said Jake.

"I agree, what caused the trap to be sprung?"

"Look at this."

Jake pointed to a tile on the floor that was depressed by the foot of the prone body. Grasping the foot with two fingers, he gingerly moved it off the tile. As the tile rose back into place, the hole in the column disappeared.

"What do we do now?" asked Qazjix.

Jake pulled out his hand-held scanner and held it over the tile.

"What do you see?"

"The density of the material below this tile is somewhat less than the surrounding tiles. I'm hoping we can use that to avoid any traps."

"A logical idea Jake, I hope you're correct."

Jake swept the device back and forth as he and Qazjix made their way out of the room and into another curved hall. As they had previously seen, after about 40 yards they came to another room. This room looked smaller than the previous room they had been in and the scanner didn't reveal any other obvious traps. As Qazjix started to step in, Jake held up his arm and stopped her.

"Hold up. Check out this rock and dust here under the archway."

"I see it, but what is its importance?"

"Look up, there's a hole here."

Jake took out his binoculars and looked at the archway exiting the room.

"Just as I thought, the same hole and the same debris. Here take a look."

Qazjix took the binoculars from Jake and saw the small hole in the archway and the bit of rock and debris on the floor underneath it.

"Watch this."

Jake picked up a rock and threw it in the middle of the room. As soon as the rock landed, the floor of the room dropped apart at the center. Jake leaned over and saw that the rock had fallen into a pit lined with spikes. Three bodies in various states of decomposition were a reminder of how deadly the trap was. While looking at the bodies, the two halves of the floor slowly rotated up until they came together and reformed into a solid floor.

"That would have been us if we had gotten out in the middle of the room."

"I'm can't believe you saw that. How did they get across?"

"I've done a bit of rock climbing before. This hole right here in the archway looks like where a piton was air gunned in. They probably shot a cable with a spike tip across and embedded it into the rock across the way. Then it was just a matter of using the cable to cross. I imagine that with Zedra's experience with tombs, she has run into many of these kinds of traps before."

"There is a certain dark genius in the design. Do you have any ideas how we can get across?"

"I think so. Notice how the floor splits very quickly, but then slowly rises back up, until both halves come together?"

"Yes."

"What if I throw another rock into the middle? As the two sides come to near horizontal position, we run across. We'd have to make it to the other side before the trap reset or we'd be skewered. What do you think? I'm certainly open to ideas."

"I don't see that we have a choice in the matter," said Qazjix as she shook her head.

"Let's do a little experiment to see exactly how much time we would have."

Jake grabbed a rock and threw it into the middle of the room. The floor sprang open and the rock fell among the spikes. Jake started counting as the two halves of the floor started rising.

"I timed it at about 15 seconds," said Jake as the floor locked back into position, "but we can't start across until ten seconds have passed or the chance of us sliding onto the spikes is too great. Can we get across in five seconds?"

"I don't see where we have a choice. I'll go first, I'm the fastest."

Jake wasn't going to argue with the Wixilan. He picked up another rock, tossed it into the middle of the room and started the count down.

"15, 14, 13, 12, 11, 10, 9, 8, 7, 6, GO!"

The muscular Wixilan bounded across the room like a gazelle. Jake held his breath and didn't let it out until she made it across with only one second to spare.

"Are you ready Jake? I can try to find some other

way of getting you across?"

"No, we don't have time. I'm faster than I look."

Jake used to be faster than he looked. The spear so kindly given to him by the Borrol on Vega Onias still caused him considerable pain whenever he had to run. Jake picked up a nearby stone and tossed it into the center of the room.

"15, 14, 13, 12, 11, 10, 9, 8, 7, 6..."

Jake's perception of time slowed as he sprinted across the room.

Five seconds.

Each step was more difficult than the last.

Four seconds.

Jake's leg started to throb.

Three seconds.

The pain was almost unbearable.

Two seconds.

Nearly to Qazjix.

One second.

The floor came together with a metallic clang. Just as Jake felt it start to fall away, he jumped, praying that he could grab the edge with his hands. As he flew through the air, the realization that he wasn't going to make it went through his mind. His thoughts were interrupted as he jerked to a stop and floated in mid-air. As Jake tried to make sense of what was happening, he realized that the world was going black.

"Jake, Jake, can you hear me?"

Jake's eyes opened to see the hazy outline of a green shape. Before he could focus, he realized that his right shoulder was on fire and he couldn't move it. Jake turned his head and realized he was lying in the hallway outside the room, with Qazjix kneeling beside him.

"What?"

"Try to relax and don't talk. I know that you must be disoriented so let me try to explain what happened. You jumped just as the floor fell inward. I was able to grab you by the hand before you fell into the pit. I'm sorry, but your shoulder dislocated when that happened. To make things worse, I had to pull you up and the only hold I had was on your hand. You passed out from the pain. I'm so very sorry, Jake."

Jake shook his head.

"No, I, uh, I'd be dead if you hadn't. How bad is it? I can't move my arm at all."

"While you were unconscious, I reset the shoulder back into the joint and made a sling with your shirt. It's not much, but it was the best I could do. I'm still so sorry. I feel terrible that I have caused you so much pain."

"It's ok. I'd much rather be in pain than be dead. You saw three bodies down there that would gladly trade places with me."

"Lay here for a few minutes and try to rest. I'll keep watch."

Jake laid still and tried to ignore the pain in his shoulder and the growing nausea it was causing him.

"Jake, maybe we should withdraw to the ship and try to radio for help."

"There's no time. At least it's my right arm, so I can still shoot with my pistol. Give me a few minutes to catch my breath."

"Take your time. I'm going to scout ahead."

"Ok, I'll try to stay quiet, but here take my extra ammo. I can't use this rifle with a busted shoulder. "

After lying on the ground for a few minutes, Jake used his left arm to push himself up to a sitting position.

"Ugggghhhh..." he grunted from the intense pain in his shoulder.

Qazjix came back from around the bend in the corridor and leaned over beside him.

"That wasn't quiet."

"Help me up. We need to keep going."

Qazjix gently lifted Jake to his feet by placing her arm underneath his uninjured shoulder. Linked together, the two crept around the corridor until coming to the entrance to another room.

"Hold up, let me scan it."

Jake pulled out the scanner and swept the room for traps.

"Nothing, let's go."

"Wait."

Qazjix took a handful of rocks and threw them into the room. Nothing happened and they continued through the room and into the next corridor. As they got close enough to the next area, they paused while Jake adjusted his sling.

Chk. Chk. Chk. Chk.

The sound came from the room just ahead.

"I think they've got a waiting party for us," whispered Jake.

"What do you want to do?"

"I can still fire a gun and we do still have these," said Jake as he pointed to the stun grenades.

"You sound like you have a plan."

"Calling it a plan is a bit of an exaggeration. I'll fire a few shots to give them something to think about. Then you pull the pins on two of the grenades and toss them in the room. Hopefully that'll disorient them and we can take them out."

"I am ready when you are."

Qazjix took two of the stun grenades from Jake. Slowly, they made their way to entrance to the next room. Jake peeked in the room but didn't see anyone.

"See anything?" asked Qazjix.

"No, but this room is like the others we have been through with the columns down both sides. I did see some footprints in the dust. They go to the far side of the room."

"Let's do this, Jake."

Qazjix positioned herself on one side of the entrance, while Jake was positioned opposite her. Jake raised his pistol and fired three shots into the room. Four men swung out from behind several of the columns to return fire. As they did, Qazjix timed her throw perfectly. The grenades found their mark and all four men were stunned. Jake grimaced in pain as he ran to the two men on the left side and shot both of them in the head. Qazjix went to the men on the right side and grabbed them both by their necks. A sharp crack emanated from both men. Qazjix let them go and their bodies fell limply to the floor.

"Nice. Could you teach me that sometime?" asked Jake.

"I don't mean this to be cruel, but you are far too physically weak a species for the technique to be effective."

"I won't argue with that. Check the bodies for anything we can use and then let's continue. It can't be that much further."

"Here are a couple of grenades," said Jake as he attached them to his belt.

"This one doesn't have anything," said Qazjix.

"Ok, let's keep going."

Jake and Qazjix entered the next curved corridor and walked about 20 yards until they came to the entrance to another room. The room was different from the others they had been through. There were no columns nor any decorative markings on the wall.

"Let me check it," said Jake as he pulled out his scanner.

While Jake scanned the room, Qazjix tossed in a few rocks for good measure.

"What do you think?"

"I think the lack of indication that there is a trap, indicates there's a trap. Hold on."

Jake hopped into the room and immediately hopped back out as a puzzled look came across Qazjix's face.

"Ok, did that look as stupid to you as it felt to me?"

Qazjix just smiled without saying a word.

"I thought that if there was a trap that I could trip it and jump back out of the way."

Qazjix kept her smile and nodded.

"Let's just hurry through the room and see if we can

make it without tripping any traps."

Jake and Qazjix sprinted through the room without incident until they got nearly to the archway exit on the opposite side of the room. Just as they were about to exit the room, a large stone block fell and blocked their exit.

"Quick, back the way we came!" yelled Jake.

They turned and sprinted toward the entranceway. Qazjix had nearly stepped under the arch when Jake grabbed her and pulled her back. As she stopped, a large stone block fell where she had just been.

"Thank you again. I would have been crushed, but how did you know?"

"It was a lucky guess. So there was a trap after all, although this one doesn't seem so bad. If we don't come out after a bit, Mikja should come and find us."

As Jake finished his sentence, a loud scraping noise started accompanied by a grinding sound.

"I think you spoke too soon Jake."

"But what is that?"

A small cloud of dust floated through the room as the noise grew louder.

"Qazjix, are you getting taller?"

"Jake, that is a fairly illogical question even for you."

Jake pointed at the ceiling. Qazjix looked up to see that the ceiling was dropping at a rate of about a foot a minute.

"Let's see if we can lift this rock blocking the exit."

Qazjix bent over and tried to put her fingers under the block without success.

"There's no way I can even get my fingers underneath the block."

Jake took out his scanner and started walking around the room.

"What are you doing?"

"I'm trying to find anything that might get us out of here. I hope the scanner can find a weak point or a trap door or something."

When the ceiling dropped low enough, Qazjix pushed her hands up against it to try to slow the descent. As Jake scanned back and forth across the room, the scanner beeped as he walked across a small square section of the floor.

"Back up to the far side of the room and cover your head, I want to try something."

Jake aimed his pistol at the spot that the scanner revealed. He fired until he had emptied the clip.

"Come over here!" yelled Jake.

Qazjix, now having to bend over at the waist, ran to Jake. He pointed to where the rifle bullets had struck the floor. A small jagged hole had formed. Jake pulled out his flashlight and shined it into the hole.

"It's hollow."

Both Jake and Qazjix fired another clip into the floor, enlarging the hole. Qazjix took the survey hammer clipped to her belt and pounded the edge of the hole. Both dropped to their knees as the ceiling kept dropping. As the space got tighter, Qazjix continued pounding the hammer around the edges, finally enlarging the hole enough to drop into. Jake shone his light back down the hole.

"Go, it looks like it's only a six foot drop."

The Wixilan crawled on her belly and dropped into the hole, feet first. She had to bend at the waist due to her being about a foot and a half taller than the space. Jake turned himself around and dropped in behind her just as the ceiling slammed into the floor.

"What do you think this is?"

The light from Jake's flashlight revealed a three-foot tall tunnel at the bottom of the shaft.

"If I had to guess, I'd say this is some kind of service tunnel. I bet if we crawl that way we'll come out in the room with the spikes that we saw. Whoever built this place, had to have a way to sharpen up those spikes and do other maintenance on these fine traps that we've run into. I know it'll be uncomfortable, but I think we need to crawl in this tunnel. Unless I miss my guess, we'll come up on one of these access points for the next room along the way."

"I trust you Jake, let's go."

Jake and Qazjix got on their hands and knees and

started crawling. Qazjix's back scraped against the top of the tunnel, but it wasn't much more comfortable for Jake. The tunnel was dry and dusty and it had the same musty smell as the rest of the place.

"I have to wonder even at a time like this how old these tunnels are. They appear to be hundreds, if not thousands of years old."

"Always the archeologist," joked Jake.

After they crawled for 40 yards, they came to another access port similar to the one they had found. Qazjix shined her light against the top of the port. It revealed a simple hinge and sliding bolt. Grabbing the bolt, Qazjix slid it open. It was a testament to whatever material it was created with, that it opened as easily as the day it was installed.

"Let's try to be as quiet as we can. There's no telling who or what's up there."

Qazjix opened the trapdoor and peered around the room. Not seeing or hearing anything, she took out her flashlight and looked around.

"It's clear."

Both climbed out of the access port and into another large hall.

"Well, the designers of this place are nothing if not consistent. With the columns and the doorways, it looks just like the other rooms," said Jake as he looked around.

Jake scanned for traps as he and Qazjix walked

across the room. No signs of anything out of the ordinary could be found, but as they reached the exit of the room they found something different. It didn't open up into another corridor, but another room. Jake and Qazjix peered into the room. Inside was pitch black except for a bright light in the center of the ceiling. The light illuminated a platform that was encircled with the same kind of jewels that were on the cylinder. The two walked into the room and up to the platform.

"Jake, there's a hole in the middle of this thing."

"I think I see how everything fits together."

"It took you long enough. Where's the walking luggage?" came a voice from the darkness above Jake.

"Zedra, I was wondering where you were. One of your goons got lucky and shot him just before I painted the wall with his brain. Don't worry though, Mikja's just fine. It was just a flesh wound."

"Too bad. Bring up the lights, gentlemen."

The entire room flooded with lights installed on a walkway near the ceiling. Zedra, Dr. Kyriakos, and Petrik Morden descended the staircase to the ground level.

"I hope your shoulder is ok," Zedra said with a smile.

"It's just fine. Let's quit the small talk," said Jake.

"Have it your way. I had a suspicion that you three would survive. So I considered it a test. Here's the deal, I can use you three. Join my group and I'll cut you in on the profits."

"You're a monster that would kill her own father. I will kill you with my bare hands," said Qazjix in a low hushed tone.

"Now, now, my dear green goliath. My father barely had time for me. What kind of life is it for a girl to be pulled from one dig to another, never putting down roots and never having friends? And then, to have a father that controls everything, forgets my birthdays and even forgets me on more than one occasion. I was nothing to him and he was nothing to me."

"You're despicable Zedra," said Jake.

"And I played you like a master would play a violin."

"So who's in charge, you or Kyriakos?"

"Let's just say it's an equitable split."

"That doesn't sound very fair to poor Petrik."

"I think you should worry about your own self, rather than trying to sow the seeds of discord. Petrik is being paid rather well."

Petrik nodded in support.

"Zedra, you need to take a closer look at this translation. This device can't be perfected. It is nothing but a weapon," said Qazjix.

"So the mindless monster thinks she can do the work of a trained professional. However, in this case, you are exactly right. I have no interest in unlimited energy, but in selling a weapon that can destroy a planet. Imagine the possibilities. Imagine the profit."

"The doctor doesn't have much to say," said Jake.

"Kyriakos is a man that knows his place," answered Zedra as she raised her weapon.

"We're going to stop you of course," said Jake.

"You can try, but first a little internal business."

Zedra swung her pistol around and placed it against Kyriakos' head.

"Your services are no longer needed."

Zedra pulled the trigger and a red spray erupted from the side of Kyriakos' head.

Jake seized the moment and threw his last stun grenade. Blinded by the intense light, Zedra and Petrik fired wildly all around. Jake traded fire with Petrik as he took cover behind the alien device. Amidst the bedlam and distraction, Qazjix ran and tackled Zedra around the waist.

"Get off me you animal!" yelled Zedra.

Qazjix responded by slapping Zedra across the face with the back of her hand. In a move that surprised her, Zedra shifted her weight and flipped Qazjix off to the side. As the effect of the stun grenade dissipated, Zedra and Petrik retreated behind the staircase of the room while Jake and Qazjix crouched behind the pedestal. Both groups trained their guns on each other.

"I think we have a standoff, Jake. If you try to leave

we'll pick you off, or have you forgotten what a good shot I am?" yelled Zedra.

"I don't think so. We have the cylinder and I'll destroy it if I have to."

"And just what are you going to do with it?"

"Watch me."

Jake stood up and slid the cylinder into the center hole. For the next few seconds, nothing happened.

"Looks like the standoff continues, Jake. It must be a bust. Why don't we both just leave and we'll forget this ever happened."

"You'll do nothing until I avenge your father," said Qazjix.

Before Jake could respond, a slight vibration started to shake the temple. The jewels on the side of the pedestal lit up one at a time, glowing softly at first and then increasing in brightness. Once one jewel reached its full intensity, the next one started to glow.

"We're leaving Zedra, I suggest you do the same."

Jake and Qazjix backed out of the room as Zedra and Petrik rushed to the pedestal. As Jake looked back, he saw Zedra attempt to remove the cylinder from the hole without success.

"Run to the ship!" Jake shouted.

The vibrations kept growing in intensity, so by the time Jake and Qazjix got to the entrance hall, it was a full-fledged earthquake. Dodging the columns as they fell, Jake and Qazjix ran out of the building and down the stairs. Once they got to the Obsidian, they bounded up the ramp and into the ship. Mikja was lying down his with leg bandaged and the open med kit beside him. Qazjix closed the ramp and sat down beside Mikja.

"Can I help you with anything?" asked Qazjix.

"No, I think I'm good. This med kit has some pretty nice painkillers. Oh, by the way, good to see you Captain."

"Good to see you too. Pardon me while I get us out of here."

"Help me up to the co-pilot's chair. This ship flies better with two people."

"You're flying pretty high already, you need to lay here."

"I didn't cauterize this wound by myself just to get blown up because we can't take off quick enough," said Mikja as he tried to sit up.

"I think Qazjix can help. You rest."

Qazjix laid Mikja back down and sat down in the co-pilot's chair.

"This won't be difficult. Just follow my lead," said Jake.

"I'll do my best."

"Fire up the null gravity field. It's that switch right

there."

Qazjix flipped the control to activate the null gravity field.

As the rocket engines glowed, the Obsidian started to float up.

"Give me maximum rocket thrust, and be ready to enter the hyperspace curve as soon as we hit orbit."

"What?"

"Sorry, I forgot. Push that lever right there, slowly up."

"Where are we going?"

"Anywhere far away. At the rate that machine was going, I figure the planet's got about two minutes left."

The Obsidian rose quickly as the rocket engines strained at their limits.

"About 50 seconds left," announced Jake.

"It's going to be close, approaching orbit. I hope you're counting fast!"

"20 seconds. Me too."

"Jake, look at the planet," yelled Qazjix.

Jake looked back at the rapidly shaking planet and the sight took his breath away. The entire planet quaked as bolts of lightning lit up the atmosphere.

"Ten seconds."

"Five seconds."

"We've reached minimum orbit and the ship is entering the hyperspace curve."

As the ship started to vibrate, Jake looked back again at the planet just as it exploded. The shockwave carrying fire and debris flew toward the Obsidian.

"It's going to be close!" said Jake.

Just as the first concussive wave reached the Obsidian, the ship jumped onto the hyperspace curve.

"Whew, I don't want to ever cut it that close again."

"I agree Jake."

"Hey Captain, maybe our next job could be a little less stressful?" shouted Mikja from the back.

"Jake, what about Zedra and Petrik? Did they get off the planet?" asked Qazjix.

"I don't know. As we ran out of the room, Zedra and Petrik were trying to remove the cylinder. They might have blasted off, but I never saw their ship. I don't know if they had time, even if they had gotten off the planet, to get far enough away to escape the shock waves."

"We can hope they didn't," said Mikja.

"Well Qazjix, the offer to join us is still open or we

can drop you on any planet you name. You've earned passage anywhere."

"I don't really have anybody left Jake. I think I will take you up on your offer, but where are we going?"

Just as Jake was about to answer, a yellow light flashed on the comm panel.

"Looks like we've got a message," said Jake as he pressed the play button.

The comm panel displayed a hologram message on the screen. A middle-aged man appeared on the screen looking worried.

"Jake old buddy, this is Ram Achok. I've got a nice milk run here that needs your special touch. Get back with me and I'll make it worth your while."

"Does that answer your question Qazjix?"

"Send a message and tell him we're going to get Mikja's leg fixed up and then we're on our way."

Ashley Sherer

Ashley Sherer

Jake Astro
and the
Island of Doom

Ashley Sherer

Jake sat in a high-backed brown leather chair as Ram Achok sat across from him behind a large wooden desk. Ram shuffled through a large stack of papers that were scattered haphazardly in front of him.

"Milk run huh? If it's so easy then why don't you take it?" asked Jake.

Ram sat back in his chair and raised his hands.

"Here I am, a nice guy trying to throw a friend a little work and I get the third degree."

Jake leaned forward.

"That might be because the last time you threw me a little work, I ended up getting busted for having a load of endangered Zynuvian taklets. That cost me 4,000 credits and 30 days probation. I don't need friends like that."

173

"Then why did you show up?"

Jake's shoulders dropped and he took a long drink from his ale.

"Mikja's going to be laid up for a couple of weeks and I'm breaking in a new co-pilot. I need something that's not going to be anything exotic."

"Yeah, I heard about that. Tough break. Good thing he didn't lose that leg."

"It would've just grown back on it's own. Damn lizard people," said Jake with a grin.

"Trust me, this one is as easy as they come."

"Give me the details."

"It's a quick cargo and passenger drop off at Jovan Superior in the Boshi system."

Jake looked at Ram with his eyebrow raised.

"What cargo and how many passengers?"

Ram smiled knowing he had piqued Jake's interest.

"I haven't taken the job yet," warned Jake.

"But you will. Listen, it's simple. All you do is drop off three passengers and some scientific equipment. That's it. You'll be taking them to an island research facility in the northern hemisphere, called Tinos."

"What kind of research facility? This isn't military is it?"

"No, they're a bunch of hippie scientists trying to save the galaxy. They do some sort of genetic experiments on crops or livestock or something."

"Giant ears of corn with legs. Mikja will hate that he missed this one. Who are the passengers?"

"Dr. Jeremy Martin, Dr. Laia Macha and Dr. Li Chang. All three are geneticists of some kind. That's all I've got."

"Just those three?"

"I knew you'd be interested."

"How much?"

"Three thousand credits minus my usual fee."

"And your usual fee this week is?"

"You really know how to hurt a guy. Only a 10% fee."

Ram lit a cigar and leaned back in his chair.

"3%" said Jake.

"7%" countered Ram as blue smoke floated out of his mouth.

"5%"

Ram leaned forward and smiled.

"Done. I'm sending the details to your computer right now."

"When do we leave?"

"I can have everything loaded and passengers at your hangar tonight."

"And the payment?"

"Half now, the other half as soon as I get notification that the cargo and passengers have been successfully delivered."

Jake stood up and extended his hand.

"Then we have a deal. I'll go get my ship ready."

Ram stood up and shook Jake's hand.

"Good doing business with you again Jake. You won't regret this."

"Famous last words."

Jake left the office and walked out into the street. The bright midday sun felt good on his face after being cooped up in Ram's dank office for so long. After he made his way out of the outdoor market located outside of Ram's front door, he jogged to the spaceport and out to where the Obsidian was. Qazjix was outside the ship making the standard inspection of the landing gear for any cracks caused by the landing on Cygnus Four.

"Jake, did we get the job?"

"Yep, we leave tonight, co-pilot."

"That is wonderful. I appreciate you taking me on

board and training me while Mikja is healing from his injuries."

"You're helping me out. I've never seen someone learn so quickly."

"Thank my genetic engineering for that. The Wixilan were bred to be able to learn tasks very quickly."

"Come on, let's get the inside of the ship fixed up. We're going to be taking three passengers with us along with the equipment."

Jake and Qazjix walked up the ramp and into the Obsidian. For the next several hours, they prepared the ship for both passengers and cargo. Jake cleaned up the passenger area while Qazjix readied the cargo hold. After a couple of hours, the cargo was delivered via robot and loaded into the cargo hold. Thirty minutes later the human cargo arrived. Jake and Qazjix stood at the top of the ramp as the three passengers waited on the spaceport floor with their luggage.

"Good evening, I'm Jake Astro your pilot. This is Qazjix, our co-pilot for the journey."

"A Wixilan? I didn't think they were good for anything but brute strength," remarked the man to the woman standing beside him.

Jake walked over to the man.

"She's very effective at that also, would you like a demonstration?"

The man's face turned bright crimson as he looked down.

"I didn't think so. Now if I can get your names?"

"I'm Dr. Martin, Dr. Laia Macha and-"

"And I can speak for myself, I'm Dr. Li Chang."

"If you will get aboard and strap in, we'll be blasting off in just a few minutes."

Dr. Martin and Dr. Macha went up the ramp and into the ship without a word. Dr. Chang stopped as she passed by Jake.

"I'm sorry for Dr. Martin's comment. He's really a brilliant scientist."

Jake didn't say a word as the women continued up the ramp to join her colleagues. Qazjix walked down the ramp and stood beside Jake.

"Thank you Jake, but it's unnecessary. It is an unfortunate part of my Wixilan heritage. Any genetically engineered species has to live with this prejudice."

"Sorry, but you're more than just a brute, you're a part of my crew. I won't let any of my crew get talked about like that. Come on and let's get underway."

Both turned and walked into the ship. After checking to ensure his passengers were strapped in and their gear was properly stored, Jake and Qazjix took their place in the cockpit. Qazjix activated the null gravity field and the ship floated upwards. Jake fired the rocket engines and within minutes the Obsidian had entered orbit around Cygnus Four. Qazjix rechecked the hyperspace curve coordinates in the computer and waited for Jake to give the word to go. Jake turned his chair around to the passenger area.

"We're ready to enter the hyperspace curve if everyone is ready."

The three passengers nodded.

"I think we're all ready to get there, Captain," said Dr. Chang.

Jake turned his chair around and entered the command into the ship's computer. The ship started to vibrate and became translucent as the hyperspace curve generator powered up. As the generator reached full power, the ship jumped onto the hyperspace curve. For the next five hours, the scientist passengers talked quietly among themselves. A red light started to flash on the control panel and Jake swung his chair around to face the passengers.

"We're approaching Jovan Superior and should be down on the ground in about half an hour."

Jake swung back around and leaned over to Qazjix.

"Would you like to get some more free fall practice time in?"

"I'd love to. Thank you Jake."

Jake spent the next few minutes taking Qazjix through the landing procedure. As she worked the controls, Jake instructed her on things to watch out for and how to 'feel' her way through while landing.

"Now, ease off on the engines. Let the null gravity drive do the work."

"I didn't realize that this was a training flight. Dr. Morbius will hear about this," complained Dr. Martin.

Jake bit his tongue as the voice from the back grated on his nerves. He had promised to teach Qazjix how to fly the Obsidian. With Mikja, still not medically cleared to fly, this seemed like the perfect opportunity. Of course that was before the assignment was expanded to include passengers.

"Mr. Martin," said Jake.

"Doctor Martin," he corrected.

"Doctor Martin, you are as safe in Qazjix's hands as you are in mine. Now if you're unhappy with the service I will allow you to disembark immediately. We're only a few thousand miles up. Do I make myself clear?"

In this case, silence equaled consent and Jake didn't hear any more comments from Martin as the ship continued its descent.

"You're doing good Qazjix, but let me take her in the rest of the way."

"Of course Jake, this is trickier than it initially looked."

"It just takes practice and you'll get a lot of practice with Mikja grounded for another two weeks."

Jake feathered the engine power down as he

adjusted the intensity of the null gravity field. The Obsidian touched down on the private spaceport on Tinos and Jake shut down the engines and null gravity field. Through the cockpit window, a small gray-haired man waited at the edge of the landing pad flanked on both sides by two robots. Qazjix lowered the ramp and the passengers disembarked onto the tarmac. He and Qazjix followed the passengers down the ramp where they were greeted by the small man and his robots.

"Welcome Captain, I'm Doctor Charles Morbius. Welcome to Tinos."

Jake shook the doctor's extended hand.

"I'm Jake Astro and this is my co-pilot Qazjix. If you'll tell us where, we'll get your equipment unloaded."

"A Wixilan. My goodness, you don't see a lot of those piloting ships. I'll bet she is tremendously talented."

Jake shook his head, "Yes she is, now if you will let us know where to put your cargo?"

Dr. Morbius gestured toward a flatbed trailer attached to the back of his transport parked on the side of the landing pad.

"If you could unload everything on to the trailer, I would certainly appreciate it."

"Of course, Doctor."

Jake and Qazjix unloaded the cargo from the hold of the Obsidian as the doctor and his robots greeted his three new colleagues. They talked as the cargo was placed onto the trailer. As Jake loaded one of the last cartons on the trailer, Dr. Morbius walked back over to him.

"Captain Astro?"

"Yes."

"I would like to extend to you the hospitality of my facility this evening. We've got a couple of extra bedrooms if you and your co-pilot would like to get a good night's sleep and a hot meal before leaving."

Jake looked at Qazjix who nodded.

"Thank you, we'd be very happy to take you up on your offer," answered Jake.

"Excellent. It looks like you are nearly done loading the equipment. We'll all ride up to the facility together."

"Give us ten more minutes and we'll be ready to go."

Jake and Qazjix finished unloading the rest of the equipment and joined the rest of the group in his transport.

"Captain, I believe you've met your passengers but allow me to introduce RT906 and RT124 to you and your co-pilot."

"Good evening. I am RT906, personal laboratory assistant to Dr. Morbius. It is my pleasure to make your acquaintance."

"And I am RT124, personal assistant to RT906. It is also my pleasure to make your acquaintance."

"We are very glad to meet you both," responded Qazjix.

"Dr. Morbius, we're awfully crowded in here. Can't the androids and the Wixilan ride on the trailer?" asked Dr. Martin.

"The Wixilan will ride with us. Perhaps you would like to ride on the trailer?" said Jake Astro.

"Sir, RT124 and I do not mind riding on the trailer."

"Thank you RT906 for the offer," said Dr. Morbius.

The two robot assistants climbed out of the transport and onto the trailer with the equipment.

"Everybody ready to go?"

"I think so, Doctor," replied Qazjix.

Dr. Morbius drove the transport up the winding road to the research facility.

"So Doctor, what kind of genetic research are you involved in here?"

"I can't say exactly, for security reasons, but if successful, it wouldn't be an exaggeration to say that it will change the galaxy."

"That's very impressive, I hope your experiments succeed."

"Why thank you, Qazjix."

The group in the transport continued to make small

talk for the 15-minute ride to the facility. As the transport pulled over a small rise, the compound came into view. A large 15ft high chain link fence with a heavy metal gate surrounded three buildings. All three buildings were the same size and shape. They were constructed with concrete block and metal roofs, painted gray. A huge circular gravel drive connected the buildings within the fence. Dr. Morbius stopped the transport at the front gate of the compound.

"Welcome to my research facility," said Morbius with a flourish.

Morbius pressed a button on the dash and the gate swung open.

"Allow me to give you a quick tour of the grounds."

The doctor drove through the gate and pulled onto the circular drive that connected all three buildings.

"This first building is the living quarters. It has six bedrooms, each with it's own private bath. There is a workout facility and a small dining hall. In addition, there is a combination library and recreational area. I don't want to sound like I'm bragging, but it's quite comfortable."

"That sounds more like a health spa rather than a government research facility," quipped Jake.

"Ahh captain, this is a private research facility. Everything here is paid for by me."

"Impressive Doctor Morbius."

"Thank you, Dr. Chang. No expense was spared.

184

Now if you notice this second building here."

The doctor pointed as the transport pulled in front of the large structure and stopped.

"This is the laboratory. I imagine most of your time will be spent here, doctors. Now, for the last building."

The doctor drove the transport and parked it in front of the final building.

"A bit anticlimactic, but here is the warehouse. Here we store everything from our supplies to spare equipment. On a different subject, I hope you're hungry. It's dinner time here at the facility."

Everyone voiced agreement as the doctor drove the transport back in front of the living quarters.

"Doctor, I notice there aren't any guards here on the island."

"Ahh, that is a mistake Dr. Martin. Allow me to demonstrate."

Morbius pressed another button on the dash of the transport. Immediately, an alarm sounded across the complex and the entrance gate slammed shut. Two heavily armed robot guards charged out of the laboratory entrance, one robot guard came out of the living facility and one robot guard came out of the warehouse. All four guards rushed to the transport and snapped to attention.

"As you can see, we are not completely left to the mercies of the criminal element here. These are HARM 900 series robots."

"HARM?" asked Dr. Macha.

"Heavily Armed Response Machines."

"They are quite frightening."

"No one asked your opinion, Macha," snapped Dr. Martin.

Jake glared at Dr. Martin.

"Something to say to me, Captain Astro?"

"Not yet, but I imagine we'll have a conversation before we leave tomorrow."

"Now, now, gentlemen. Perhaps dinner will calm you both down."

The six people exited the transport and waited by the door to the living facility.

"RT906 and RT124, take the transport and the trailer and park them in the warehouse," ordered Dr. Morbius.

"Yes sir," both RT units answered in unison.

RT906 got in the driver's seat as RT124 stayed on the trailer. RT906 drove the transport to the warehouse as the group walked into the living facility. Doctor Morbius stepped in front of the group to address them.

"The dining room is here to the left. The library and recreation center is off to the right. Along this hall are the living quarters. My quarters are here in the first room. For simplicity, Dr. Martin, Dr. Macha, and Dr. Chang can take the three remaining rooms on this side. Captain Astro, you and Qazjix can use the first two rooms on the right. I think you'll find everything you need already in the room. However, don't hesitate to let me know if you are lacking anything."

"Thank you Doctor," said Qazjix.

"Dinner will be in one hour. Feel free to take advantage of the library and rec center or just rest in your rooms."

Jake went into his room and had been there for about ten minutes when he heard a knock on the door.

"Jake, it's Qazjix, may I come in?"

"Of course."

Qazjix opened the door and walked in. She pressed her finger against her lips and walked over to a lamp located on the nightstand beside the bed. As she picked up the lamp, she motioned Jake to come closer and take a look. There was a small listening device attached to the bottom of the lamp. Jake nodded.

"It's a beautiful facility Jake. I think I'm going to take a quick walk on the oval grass area outside. Would you like to join me?"

"I would love to. A good walk will do wonders for my appetite."

Jake and Qazjix exited the room and out the main

doors. They walked for several minutes before Qazjix spoke.

"I was putting my things away when I accidentally knocked over the lamp. That's when I saw the listening device. I thought I should see what you thought about it."

"They could be in all the rooms because this is a high security facility and the good doctor doesn't want any secrets slipping out. We're out of here tomorrow morning as soon as possible and we'll let our passengers deal with it."

"Shouldn't we tell them about it?"

"I don't see where it's any of our business. We're just delivery men, excuse me, delivery persons."

"I don't like that Jake. It feels dishonest."

"Look, if it makes you feel any better about it, I'll hint around it at dinner tonight. If we get bad vibes, we'll tell everybody before we leave and if they want they can hitch a ride back."

Qazjix smiled.

"Thank you Jake, you're a good man."

"Don't spread it around. Ready to go eat?"

"I'm famished."

The two turned and walked back to the living quarters and entered the dining hall. The rest of the group was just being seated.

"Ahh, just in time Captain Astro. I trust you and Qazjix have worked up an appetite with your stroll across the grounds."

"I think so Doctor," said Jake taking his seat in between Qazjix and Dr. Chang.

"Excellent, and did you come to any conclusions about the bugging devices found in your room?"

Jake nearly knocked over his water glass in surprise.

"You knew about that, and you admit it?"

"Why of course, and I must apologize to you. Everyone's room has a video camera and multiple listening devices. You must understand it's part of the employment contract for anyone working here. I admit, I forgot all about them when I assigned you your rooms."

Jake turned to Dr. Chang. "You knew about this beforehand and you still wanted to come work here."

"Captain Astro, for those of us in this business where secrecy is at a premium, this is standard operating procedure," interrupted Dr. Martin.

"I appreciate the hospitality, but we'll be leaving tonight Dr. Morbius," Jake and Qazjix began to stand up.

"Please stay. I will order RT124 to disable all security devices in your rooms. Accept my most humble apologies."

Jake looked at Qazjix and nodded his head. They both sat back down.

"I guess we're just not used to the idea of corporate espionage. Are you three really ok with this?"

"It's a fairly standard practice for a project of this importance. I think I can speak for all three of us when I say the pay is well worth any loss of privacy," said Dr. Li Chang.

At that moment, RT906 rolled in a large cart filled with plates.

"RT906, please disable all security devices in our guest's rooms for the duration of their stay," ordered Dr. Morbius.

"Thank you Doctor," said Qazjix.

"You're welcome, and now for the most important part of the evening. I obviously didn't know your meal preferences ahead of time Captain Astro and Qazjix, but I think I've made pretty good guesses."

RT906 sat a plate with a medium rare steak and fried potatoes in front of Jake.

"Pretty good guess, Doc. Thanks."

"You're welcome and I think you'll enjoy your Yat, Qazjix. Prepared extra rare."

A large smile appeared on Qazjix's face as RT906 put the plate down in front of her.

"I don't think I've heard of Yat. What is that? Some sort of bird?" asked Dr. Macha.

"More like a rodent," answered Jake.

"You mean a rat?" asked Dr. Macha.

"Well, when prepared properly..." Jake left it at that and began to cut into his steak.

The color drained from Dr. Macha's face as RT906 gave everyone else's plate to them. Everyone ate quietly for the next several minutes, until Doctor Morbius stood up with his wine glass in hand.

"A toast to a new beginning and a brave new world."

"Here, here," echoed Dr. Martin.

The group at the table all raised their glasses to the toast.

The rest of the dinner went quietly and when all had finished, Doctor Morbius turned to the three other doctors.

"I think we should have a quick meeting to discuss the upcoming days. Jake, you and Qazjix can retire to your rooms. I'm sure you will want to get an early start tomorrow morning."

"I agree. Doctor, thanks for the hospitality. Qazjix?"

"I'm done as well. Thank you doctor. You have made this a most interesting evening."

Jake and Qazjix excused themselves as Dr. Morbius and the others discussed the plans for the next few days. They exited the dining hall and went back to the corridor where their rooms were located.

"This is one place I'll be glad to get away from."

"I agree. Something about this place makes me feel uneasy."

"Let's try and get away as soon as possible tomorrow morning. Is 0600 hours ok?"

"I'll be up and ready to go by then."

Jake went into his room and closed the door. Once undressed, he stretched out on the bed. The next thing Jake knew, a bright light shone into his room. It took Jake a few seconds to realize that it was the sun that blinded him. He must have been more tired than what he thought because he didn't even set his alarm. Jake looked at his watch. It read 0735. He stood up and got a quick shower, before dressing. As he sat on his bed putting on his shoes, there was a knock at his door.

"Come in."

Qazjix walked into the room dressed in the clothes she had worn last night.

"I'm sorry Jake, I must have overslept. You should have awakened me."

"No need to apologize, I overslept also. I must have been so tired I didn't even set my alarm."

"Me too."

"You don't think that..." Jake stopped when he remembered about the listening devices. He knew what Doctor Morbius said, but why take the chance.

"We must have just been really tired. Let's get to the

ship and get home," Jake continued.

The look on Qazjix's face showed that she understood what Jake was thinking.

"I agree, let's head home. I can't wait to get more flying time in."

Jake and Qazjix exited his room and went into the main entrance hall where RT124 stood.

"Good morning sir. Doctor Morbius instructed me to wait here until you emerged from your rooms and apologize that he is not here to see you off personally. He also instructed me to drive you to your ship and provide anything else that you may require."

"Thank you RT124, I think we're ready to go to my ship now."

"Excellent sir. Please follow me, I've taken the liberty of parking the transport in the front of the building."

Jake and Qazjix followed the robot out of the building and got into the transport. They kept quiet as the robot navigated the winding road down to the landing pad where the Obsidian was parked.

"Thank Dr. Morbius for the hospitality," said Qazjix.

"Yes, please thank him," added Jake with a smirk.

"You are most welcome sir. Have a safe trip."

The robot climbed back into the transport and pulled away, driving up the road that led to the compound. Jake entered the access code into his communicator and the entrance ramp lowered from the ship. He and Qazjix walked aboard as the ramp closed behind them. Sitting down in the cockpit, Jake turned to Qazjix.

"I didn't want to say anything while we were there, but did you notice anything odd about last night?"

Qazjix shrugged. "Not really, other than I fell asleep faster than normal."

"Yes, me too. I fell asleep so fast I didn't even set my alarm."

"What are you thinking Jake?"

"I think the doctor didn't trust us and we were drugged so that there wouldn't be a chance of us getting up during the night."

"But why?"

"It could be just as simple as the security around the doctor's projects. I've seen people like him who are paranoid about their work. But I could be wrong. I hope I am anyway. Are you ready to lift us off, future pilot?" Jake winked at Qazjix.

"I am now."

Qazjix's smile beamed as she went through the preflight checks.

"Preflight checks are complete and we are ready to depart," reported Qazjix.

"Take us up."

"Starting the null gravity generator."

As the engines started to glow white, the Obsidian floated upwards into the clear blue sky.

"Activating the rocket engines for trip into orbit."

As Qazjix activated the engines, there was a slight vibration. Suddenly, an alarm rang in the cockpit and a red light flashed on the console. A warning voice came over the loudspeaker.

"Atmosphere scrubber complete failure. Recommend immediate landing. Carbon dioxide levels increasing."

"Have I done something?" asked Qazjix.

"No, this is an occupational hazard of a ship this old. We better take it back down and see if we can fix it."

"What happens if we can't fix it?"

"We'll have to replace it, which could be a problem. We don't have a spare."

"What do we do then?"

"Live off the kindness of strangers. We'll have to impose on the good doctor for a little while longer," explained Jake with a reassuring grin on his face.

"Let's hope we can fix it."

"I agree. Would you like to take us back down?"

"Absolutely."

Qazjix feathered down the ship until it came to sit softly back on the landing pad.

"You're going to make a terrific pilot," said Jake.

"Thank you. If so, it's because I had an excellent teacher."

"Flattery will get you everywhere. Tell the computer to run a full diagnostic on all systems and we'll get under the ship and put eyes on the scrubbers."

Qazjix entered the command into the computer and then she and Jake exited down the ramp.

"Where are the scrubbers located?" asked Qazjix.

"On the Obsidian there are two sets of scrubbers on each side of the ship," said Jake as he walked over to the ones on the left side. He undid the clamps holding the protective plating in place. As he did, a fine black powder fell all over him.

"I guess I see the problem," declared Jake.

"What's that powder?"

"It's the material inside the scrubbers. If you see this black powder, you know you have to replace the scrubber. There's no way to fix it."

Qazjix wiped the powder out of Jake's hair.

"Thanks," said Jake as he chuckled.

"Something is funny?"

"You're just about as different from Mikja as

possible. He'd be talking about how the powder, now that's it's been exposed to my skin, will do something terrible to me."

"You are probably correct. Should we check the second scrubber?"

"Yeah, but I'm not going to get my hopes up."

Jake and Qazjix inspected the other scrubber and as their luck was going, it too had busted.

"Let me try and get the compound on the communicator. Maybe they can send someone to pick us up."

Jake took his communicator out of his pocket. His attempts to contact the compound yielded nothing but static.

"What now, Jake?"

"We hike back up to the compound and see if the good doctor has a couple of spare scrubbers?"

"Do you trust him?"

"No, but he's our only way off this planet."

"What if he doesn't have any spare scrubbers we can use?"

"I'll send a subspace message and get one delivered."

"But a subspace message will take a week to get there."

Jake gave Qazjix the thumbs up sign.

"Yep, another week with the doctor."

After packing up a few essentials, including his pistol, and securing the ship, they hiked up the winding road to the compound.

"Whew, this hike is fun."

"Your face is awfully red and you're dripping with sweat. Have you been behind the pilot's controls for too long?"

Jake laughed, but didn't waste the energy responding. As he hiked the terrain, it gave Jake a new appreciation for mechanized transport. The trail featured mountains on the ocean side and a dense green jungle on the inland side. The mountains were ugly plain granite, almost as if some god of boredom decided to go all out with his most boring creation. In contrast, the jungle was a different story. It was dense and full of vegetation of every color. You couldn't see two feet into it, but you could smell it.

"You know I could do without that stench," complained Jake.

"I like it. It reminds me of home."

They had walked halfway up to the compound when Jake heard a rustle somewhere close to the trail out in the jungle. He unsnapped the catch on his holster and was about to warn Qazjix when she turned around to him.

"There's something big out there," warned Qazjix.

"I was just about to mention it."

"We should hurry, I don't know what life is indigenous to this island. Do you?"

"Uh, no. I think I missed that day in biology class," joked Jake.

Jake and Qazjix quickened their pace when Jake noticed the rustle approaching the edge of the path.

"Can you hear that?" asked Qazjix.

"Hear what? I don't hear anything, but the same jungle sounds that we've been hearing since starting on this road."

"I forget my hearing is much more sensitive than a human's. There's a low pitched hum out there, but I can't place the source."

"I can't hear anything, but we need to get out of here quick. I want to get to that compound."

Jake broke out into a sprint up the path.

"Wait Jake!" yelled Qazjix as she ran after him.

Qazjix quickly caught up to Jake and matched him stride for stride.

"Why are you running?"

"We have to get to the compound, NOW!"

Qazjix didn't question Jake, but kept beside him until they came to the gate surrounding the complex. Jake took out his pistol and started banging on the gate.

"Doctor, let us in!"

Qazjix put her arm around Jake. He shrugged her off.

"Don't touch me, we need to get inside," he barked.

While Jake pounded on the fence, his face changed from someone almost possessed back to his normal countenance. As he breathed heavily, Jake put his pistol back into the holster and turned to Qazjix.

"I'm, uh, sorry. I don't know what was wrong with me. I just was filled with the urge that we had to get off that road."

"It's alright Jake. Are you feeling ok now?"

"I think so, but I swear, I've not been that scared in a long time."

"I don't think I've ever seen you frightened."

"Uh, it doesn't make sense," said Jake as he bent over with his hands on his knees.

"It's ok, you just got unnerved by the scrubbers going out and then the jungle setting. It could happen to anyone."

"Perhaps, can you still hear that hum?"

"Why no, I can't. Do you?"

Qazjix was interrupted by RT124 arriving on the compound transport.

"Good evening sir. It is most pleasant to see you again. How may I be of service?"

"We had a problem with our ship that prevents us from leaving. Is there anyway we can talk with Dr. Morbius?" asked Qazjix.

"I'm terribly sorry to hear that sir. If you would like, please climb aboard the transport and we will find Dr. Morbius."

The compound gate slid open and Jake and Qazjix sat down in the transport.

"Ready sir and madam?"

"Yes, RT124. Thank you," replied Qazjix.

RT124 drove the transport around the gravel drive and parked it outside the laboratory building.

"Please wait here and I will go inside and retrieve the doctor."

RT124 exited the vehicle and went inside the building.

"How do you feel, Jake?"

"I'm better, but still a little shook up."

"I'm a worried about you."

"Now, you'll make me blush," said Jake as he winked at Qazjix.

Before Qazjix could respond, the doctor came out of the laboratory and walked up to the transport.

"RT124 indicated that your ship has had some problems?"

"We've had a failure of our atmosphere scrubbers. I hoped that you might have a couple we could borrow?" asked Jake.

"I'm afraid we don't have anything like that you could use in a spaceship. Is there anything else I could help with?"

"I hate to ask, but can we send a subspace message and stay here until replacement scrubbers can be delivered?"

"Of course you can. I'm afraid that the laboratory is off limits to you, but otherwise you can have the run of the place. In fact, you can have your rooms back. With the security equipment still disabled, I assure you."

"Thank you Doctor."

"I'll have RT124 drive you over to the living quarters."

Jake shook his head.

"Thanks doc, but we can walk. Too much riding will make us lazy."

Jake and Qazjix stepped out of the transport and walked over to the living quarters.

As they walked, Qazjix turned to Jake, "Can we trust him to do what he says about keeping the security cameras off?"

"No, they'll be left on. We'll be watched and listened to every minute of the day that we're here."

Qazjix stopped.

"But why would he tell us that?" she asked.

"He wants to keep an eye on us and he can't do that if we're on the ship. Keep walking, we don't want to tip them off."

"Why don't we just stay on the ship?"

"Because I want to keep an eye on him. Something strange is going on here. Both scrubbers shouldn't have died at the same time like that."

"You think they sabotaged us?"

"I do, and if they want us to stay, I want to be close enough to keep an eye on them. Keep your eyes open, but don't say anything until we are able to get out of the range of the listening devices."

Jake opened the door to the living quarters and he and Qazjix walked in.

"Why don't you relax for awhile in your room? Maybe try and catch some sleep. I'm going to take a look at the library," suggested Jake.

"That sounds good, I am tired. Will you wake me for dinner?"

"Certainly, sleep well."

Qazjix went into her room and closed the door while Jake walked down the hall to where the doors to the library and exercise rooms were located.

"Maybe I have been in the pilot's seat for too long," said Jake as he went into the exercise room.

It was a large room with exercise equipment on one side and a small two-lane pool on the other. In addition, there was a door to a sauna and a whirlpool. He picked up a 10 pound dumbbell and did a few curls before putting the dumbbell back down.

"That should do it," he said to himself again as he left the exercise room and went into the library.

It was a traditional old-fashioned library with walls 20 feet high and full of books from floor to ceiling. In the middle of the room were several reading tables and a few computer terminals. Jake walked to the nearest shelf and ran his hand over the spines of the books. Most of the titles were in languages that Jake didn't recognize, but a few were in the common intergalactic language. Jake picked one up that caught his eye, 'Genetics and Man' by Jinson and carried it back to his room. As he sat on his bed, he thumbed through the yellowed pages. This was not a book that would ever make it into Jake's personal library. He wished he had paid more attention in some of his science classes instead of dreaming about flying or the blonde next to him. What was her name, he wondered?

"EEEEEEEEEEEEEEEEEEEEEEEEEEEE"

Jake grabbed his pistol and dashed out into the hall, beating Qazjix by only a couple of seconds.

"That was a scream," said Jake.

"Where did it come from?"

"I think outside."

Jake and Qazjix ran through the doors of the living quarters and out onto the paved drive.

"HALT OR YOU WILL BE INCAPACITATED."

Jake and Qazjix froze in their path and turned to face the source of the warning. In front of them stood one of the HARM 9000 robot guards with its rifle trained on both of them.

"RETURN TO YOUR ROOMS. THERE IS NOTHING TO SEE. RETURN TO YOUR ROOMS OR YOU WILL BE INCAPACITATED."

"What was that scream?" demanded Jake.

"RETURN TO YOUR ROOMS. THERE IS NOTHING TO SEE. RETURN TO YOUR ROOMS OR YOU WILL BE INCAPACITATED."

"Jake, what do we do?"

"We go back to our rooms. These robots are bad business."

"Jake, that was a scream. We can't just wait in our rooms."

Jake shrugged as he put his arm on Qazjix's shoulder.

"Come on."

Qazjix cast a cool gaze at Jake as they walked into the living quarters.

Jake turned toward Qazjix.

"Before you say anything, there's nothing we could do. Those robot guards would take us out before we could blink. I hate to say it, but for tonight, let's just stay in our rooms and try to get some sleep."

"I'll go to my room, but I don't think I'll get much sleep."

"Lock your door and take this."

Jake offered his pistol to Qazjix who shook her head.

"I don't mean to demean you when I say this, but you need that more than me."

"You're probably right. We'll get answers tomorrow, I promise."

"I know, Jake. Good night."

"Good night."

Jake spent a restless night tossing and turning in his bed and was relieved when he saw the sun rise the following morning. His knees and back popped as he stretched.

"You're an old man, Jacob Astro," said Jake to himself as he walked out into the hall and to Qazjix's room. Jake rapped on the door.

"Qazjix, this is Jake."

The door opened and Qazjix stood before him dressed and ready to go.

"I guess I didn't wake you."

"I've been up for a while. I have to confess I didn't sleep very well last night."

"Neither did I, let's go get some answers."

The sound of metal steps behind them, made Jake and Qazjix whirl around.

"I apologize if I startled you. Dr. Morbius requests your presence in the dining hall," said RT124.

Jake and Qazjix followed the robot into the hall where Dr. Morbius sat at the head of the table. Dr. Martin was to his right and Dr. Chang was to his left. None of them looked like they had slept last night and Dr. Chang's eyes were red and puffy as if she had been crying.

"What the hell is going on Morbius? I want some answers."

"Have a seat, please. Both of you."

"We can stand," said Jake, his arms crossed.

"Please."

Jake looked at Qazjix and the both sat down at the table.

"I know you have questions about last night."

"You bet we do. I understand we're guests, but I

don't appreciate your armed guards forcing us back into our rooms after hearing a scream."

"You have every right to feel that way. I would have felt the same way if I were you."

"You don't deny it was a scream?" asked Qazjix.

"No, of course not. Last night-"

"Dr. Macha?" Qazjix interrupted.

"Yes, there was an... accident."

The pause made Jake shiver.

"Why the pause Doctor?"

"I'm not a heartless monster. I didn't know Dr. Macha very well, but she was a colleague."

"Tell us what happened," said Jake.

"Dr. Macha was working with a sample of highly toxic bacteria. There was a containment failure and she was infected. Unfortunately, there was nothing we could do and she died within minutes," answered Dr. Martin.

Dr. Chang shot Dr. Martin a glance, but then quickly looked back down.

"You won't mind us viewing the body then?" asked Jake.

"I'm afraid that won't be possible. Because of the extremely dangerous nature of the bacteria, we were forced to disintegrate the body."

"That's very convenient, Doctor," said Jake.

"It's standard protocol when dealing with highly infectious substances. Would you rather take a chance on a plague sweeping the island and killing everyone on it and worse, everyone who lands here? Where did you go to medical school?" challenged Dr. Martin.

Jake stood and took two steps toward Dr. Martin before Qazjix stepped in between them.

"You don't want to do this Jake. We have bigger problems," said Qazjix under her breath.

Jake took a step back and winked at Qazjix.

"Of course. It's all a bit much for me. I want to apologize Dr. Martin. This has been a very stressful couple of days."

"It's quite all right. You're not used to dealing with such sophisticated things," said Dr. Martin.

Jake turned toward Dr. Morbius.

"I think we'll be staying in the Obsidian for the rest of our time here."

"Don't you think you'd be more comfortable here?"

"Possibly, but it's a bit too sophisticated for me."

"Well, should you change your mind, you both are welcome."

"Thank you, Doctor."

Jake and Qazjix walked back to their rooms and packed. As they went into the foyer, they found Dr. Chang waiting for them.

"You need to leave this island as soon as you can. There is more going on here than you could ever imagine."

"What's going on? You can come with us if it's that bad."

"I can't, but stay in your ship and don't leave it until your parts get dropped off. Then, if you're smart, you'll leave as soon as you can and not look back."

As Jake was about to reply, Dr. Morbius leaned out of the dining hall doors.

"Dr. Chang, we could use your opinion on a matter."

"Good luck. I hope you are comfortable on your ship. It was a pleasure to meet the both of you," said Dr. Chang with a forced smile.

"Dr. Chang, this is important," said Morbius.

All three exchanged handshakes before Dr. Chang went back into the dining hall while Jake and Qazjix walked outside. RT906 awaited in the transport to drive them to the Obsidian.

"Ladies first," said Jake as he gestured to the transport.

"Thank you, Jake."

Both climbed into the vehicle and RT906 started on

the trek down the hill. There was no conversation as Jake and Qazjix stared out at the island landscape as they headed back to the ship. When they reached the landing pad, RT906 parked the transport beside the Obsidian.

"Sir, may I help you with anything?" inquired RT06.

"You could tell me what's really going on here?"

"I'm sorry sir, I don't believe I understand the question."

"Never mind. Take care of yourself."

"Thank you sir."

RT906 drove away as Jake and Qazjix walked onto the ship.

"So Jake, I didn't ask before, but where do we sleep?"

"Pick a chair, any chair, or you can bunk on the floor. We took out the crew quarters and transformed it into additional cargo space. I guess I should have told you that before coming down here."

"It's not a problem Jake, I just hope my snoring doesn't keep you up."

"If I can sleep through Mikja's wheezing and hissing, I don't think it will be a problem."

Jake was never more wrong in his life. As Qazjix slumped in her chair, the frightful noise thundered through the ship. Jake swore that the sound caused the walls to shake. After six hours of fitful, restless sleep, Jake was ecstatic to see the sunrise and Qazjix begin to stir.

"Good morning Jake," said Qazjix as she stretched her arms and legs

"Good morning."

"Did you sleep well?"

"Absolutely."

"You don't lie very well. I tried to warn you."

"Yes you did and I was foolish enough not to believe you. Are you ready to learn a few more things while we're waiting on the parts? I've got to warn you, it's pretty boring."

"I'm ready. Let's get started."

Their breakfast learning session extended through the morning and into the afternoon. Jake was amazed at Qazjix's ability to learn as he went through the many intricate details of the ship's systems.

"How about we go outside and walk around the ship? We can look at some of the things we've been talking about."

"That's a great idea. I really do appreciate you taking the time to show me these things."

"I'm happy to. You're the quickest learner I've ever seen."

"You can thank my genetic breeding for that."

"There are a lot of good things about that. You have a lot of advantages in being a Wixilan."

Qazjix slumped a bit into her chair.

"There are a lot of disadvantages."

"Such as?"

"Since we are a genetically bred race, there is a lot of prejudice against us. People think we aren't really alive. More than once we've been accused of being monsters. Plus you throw in that we do have a predisposition toward rages, it's not always easy."

"But you've never shown that."

"I have worked for years through meditation and study to bring my inner demons under control. It can be a constant struggle."

Jake didn't say anything, but smiled sympathetically as he and Qazjix walked out of the Obsidian. He had just started to explain the housing of the null gravity drive when Qazjix tapped him on the shoulder.

"It looks like we have company," she said.

Jake glanced up and saw the black transport from the Morbius compound coming down the hill toward the landing pad.

"Hmm, I wonder what they want now?"

Jake continued his explanation of the null gravity housing maintenance procedures when Qazjix gripped his shoulder.

"There's something wrong."

Jake looked again at the hill. The transport, which had been driving straight down the hill, had started to weave back and forth across the road.

"What the hell are they doing? If they don't stop, they're going to run off the..."

Jake's words were interrupted as the transport went too far to the left and the driver over corrected. The transport shot back across the road and went into the runoff ditch that ran down the opposite edge and landed on its side.

"Come on!" yelled Jake as he took off toward the wrecked car. Even with a head start, Qazjix quickly outdistanced him and made it to the transport before him. She climbed up on the transport, careful to avoid the still spinning front tire in the air, and peered into the driver's window.

Qazjix turned to Jake who was just arriving at the wreck and yelled, "Hand me your knife!"

Jake took a small knife out of his pocket and tossed it up to her. Qazjix unfolded the blade and ducked her head and arms inside the cab of the vehicle. After a few seconds, Jake saw her arm come out of the cab.

"Knife!" Qazjix yelled as she tossed it in the air out of the cab. As Qazjix backed out of the transport, she pulled a body out of the cab and laid it down on the ground.

Jake joined Qazjix as they knelt down by the body. It was barely recognizable as it was covered in blood from the head to toe. Large gashes had been made across the chest, back and legs. In addition, the right side of the face was crushed in.

"It's Dr. Martin," said Qazjix as she tried to staunch the bleeding by applying pressure to the wounds.

Jake stripped off his shirt and stuffed it into the large deep wound across his chest. Blood bubbled out of his mouth as he tried to speak. Dr. Martin raised his arm slightly and gestured for Jake and Qazjix to come closer.

"This is..." slurred Dr. Martin.

"Shh. Don't talk you've been in a wreck."

"This is out of control. Help us. Help..." with that last word, Dr. Martin closed his eyes and stopped breathing.

Jake looked at Qazjix and said, "That wreck didn't cause this."

"We have to go help them."

"We need to lock ourselves into the ship and wait for those scrubbers."

"Jake."

"Ok, but we get the rifles and the pistols from the Obsidian before we head up there."

"What about the handheld scanners?"

Jake's face turned a light shade of red.

"We didn't really have enough money for fuel even with the advance for this job. I had to hock them. I thought that I could get them back when we got paid. I didn't want to tell you."

"Men and their pride," said Qazjix shaking her head.

"I know, I know. Go grab the guns while I stand watch out here to make sure we don't get any other surprises from the compound."

Without a word, Qazjix stood up and bounded into the ship. After about a minute, Jake saw her rush out carrying the weapons and something else. He didn't realize what it was until she got next to him. Handing Jake the weapons and holsters, she unfolded a sheet and gently laid it over the body. After covering the body from head to toe, she tucked the edges of the sheet underneath the body so it wouldn't blow away. As she stood, she spoke something that Jake couldn't understand.

"Ready?" asked Qazjix.

Jake handed a rifle and pistol to Qazjix after he strapped on his shoulder holster and flipped the safety on his rifle.

"Ready."

As Jake and Qazjix started the walk up the hill toward the compound, they kept watch on the jungle to ensure nothing could surprise them. After the 30-minute hike, they came over the rise before the compound. Jake was startled at the sheer carnage that they saw. The front gate had been ripped off its hinges and lay in a crumpled heap. After walking through where the gate used to be, Jake bent over the torso of one of the HARM 9000 robots.

"Anything that could do this is bad news. If you see anything, don't hesitate to shoot."

Qazjix nodded.

"Where should we start?"

"Might as well get it over with and try the lab first."

When they got to the lab, they found the door had been forced open from the inside and was lying on the ground. It had been crumpled like it was made of tin foil. Once inside, they walked down a long white corridor whose walls had been splattered with blood.

"I've got a bad feeling about this," said Qazjix.

"Stay cool and just don't shoot me."

"No problem."

At the end of the corridor was a set of double doors with a sign above them reading 'Primary Lab'. Jake pushed one of the doors open slightly and peered inside. The lab looked like a bomb had exploded. Tables and chairs had been overturned and broken; shards of glass were everywhere and blood spatter covered large portions of the walls and floors. A large cylinder propped against the wall appeared to have ruptured; as it's metal walls were forced outward.

"Come on, let's take a closer look."

They walked in, rifles drawn, moving through the room. As they came to an overturned desk in the corner against the wall, Jake noticed blood trickling out from underneath.

"Help me move this desk."

They grabbed the corner of the desk and pulled it away from the wall. Qazjix gasped as they saw the mangled, ripped apart bodies of Dr. Morbius and Dr. Chang. She checked both bodies for a pulse, but they were long dead. Qazjix pointed toward the metal cylinder.

"Do you think that container exploded and caused all this?"

Jake walked over to it and took a closer look.

"I don't think so. This metal doesn't show any burn marks. Something was in there and forced it's way out."

Qazjix searched the room looking for some clue to what had happened when she found a computer that had been thrown to the floor. She turned it over and found that it was still on and functioning.

"Jake, come look at this."

'Day 1: Embryo created from genetic source material. Placed into nutrient solution at 35 degrees Celsius. We have hopes that this will finally be the one.'

"Go forward a few pages," said Jake.

'Day 10: S103 has passed now through eight distinct development stages. Weight is approximately 22 kilos, height is 1.25 meters. It is showing remarkable

healing powers. We have introduced many biological hazards and the creature's immune system is impervious to them all.'

'Day 14: S103 has tripled in size. I have decided to name my creation, diabolus hominem. I doubt the others, when they arrive will appreciate it. It's skin has shown to be impervious to heat and injury. We will continue the treatments to try to increase its resistance to cold. We have successfully been able to allow the creature to roam the jungle and follow our commands.'

"Diabolus hominem?" asked Qazjix.

"It means Devil Man. This guy was sick. Skip on ahead," said Jake.

'Day 25: Supplies have arrived. The doltish captain and his freak co-pilot have agreed to spend the night. Neither looks like a threat...'

"Doltish Captain?" asked Jake.

"I guess the doctor was right about a few things."

"You're sounding more like Mikja every day. Why don't we continue?"

'I am overjoyed at the progress of the S103. A new ability has manifested itself as predicted. The creature can produce an ultra low frequency sound that will frighten and disorientate anyone who nears it. Daily outings continue to be an excellent opportunity to test the creature's capabilities. I don't want to prematurely declare this a success, but S103 has surpassed all previous experiments.'

"That explains our first day. That thing was in the jungle."

They left unsaid how unprotected they were that day as they walked up the hill to the compound.

'Day 28: We continue to see growth at a rate of one to three kilos a day. My colleagues are afraid that S103 is showing signs of becoming uncontrollable. I agree with them that its aggressive nature does make control more difficult. However, I am confident we can guide it as we wish, even after the regrettable incident with Dr. Macha.'

"That's the last page," said Qazjix as she looked up at Jake.

"This thing scares me."

"It scares me too, Jake. It's out there somewhere."

"I didn't think anything could scare you."

"I'm strong Jake, but anything strong enough to tear through that metal is beyond me."

"Let's keep going."

Jake and Qazjix turned to walk out when the double doors flew off the hinges and were knocked into the room. The sight in the doorway left Jake and Qazjix numb. The creature was as tall as Qazjix, but far more muscular. It had no hair and its skin was dark gray. Instead of hands, it had long claws that were at least six inches in length. The eyes were fiery red and its razor sharp teeth showed when the creature opened its mouth. Simultaneously, Jake and Qazjix raised their rifles and fired.

"The bullets have no effect!"

"Watch out Qazjix, it's coming at you!"

The massive hulk bounded over an overturned desk with amazing speed and flung Qazjix into the wall, knocking her unconscious. The creature then turned his attention to Jake who had continued to fire his rifle until the clip emptied. Jake backed away as it stalked toward him. The monster opened its mouth, but instead of a roar there was an almost inaudible rumble. After a few seconds, Jake felt the same panic and fear that he experienced walking up the path from the Obsidian to the compound. As his fear grew, he turned and ran straight into the wall behind him. In his panic, something red to his left caught his eye. It was a fire extinguisher. As certain death moved closer, Jake grabbed the extinguisher and sprayed it into the face of the monster. White smoke engulfed it as it let out a roar and ran out of the room. Jake carried the extinguisher with him as he ran to where Qazjix fell and knelt over her. As he cradled her head in his lap, he examined her to see how serious her injuries were. She was bleeding from several scratches and had a knot on the back of her head, but nothing was broken. Looking around, Jake found a beaker on the floor that was unbroken and filled it from a faucet in the corner. He poured the water along her lips and splashed her face. The water had the desired effect as her eyes fluttered until she regained consciousness.

"Don't try to move. What hurts?"

"What doesn't hurt?" said Qazjix with a smile.

"Ha, ha," Jake deadpanned, "seriously, is anything

broken?"

"No, help me up," said Qazjix as she extended her hand.

Jake stood up and took her hand. It took all his strength, but he helped Qazjix to her feet.

"Lean on me until you get your legs under you."

"Thanks Jake. Where is the creature?"

"I was able to drive him off with this," said Jake holding up the fire extinguisher.

"But how?"

"The compressed gas in it is extremely cold. I was lucky enough to spray it in that thing's face. It fled, at least for the time being."

"We better get out of here, there's no telling when it will be back," said Qazjix.

"Let's check the warehouse. I noticed it wasn't damaged like the living quarters and the lab. Perhaps we can find some more extinguishers, or maybe we can barricade that thing out. I'm hoping it's gone back to the jungle to recover."

"I agree."

Jake and Qazjix made their way out of the lab room and to the outside. Qazjix had recovered sufficiently from the attack and could walk without leaning on Jake. When they reached the warehouse, Jake opened the door trying to be as quiet as he could. Jake half expected the creature to jump out and attack them.

"Do you see any sign of that thing?" asked Qazjix.

"No, nothing. I don't think it's here."

Jake and Qazjix went into the supply warehouse and closed the door behind them.

"I'm going to lock the door, for all the good it will do," said Qazjix.

"Spread out and see if there's anything that we can use," suggested Jake.

Both he and Qazjix went searched most of the small warehouse without success. Jake had about given up when Qazjix yelled for him.

"Jake, come here!"

"What did you find?" he replied as he made his way over to Qazjix.

Qazjix pointed proudly at her find. The small gray steel tank was three feet around and five feet tall with the words 'Liquid Nitrogen' stenciled on the side. Additionally, there was a nozzle at the bottom of the tank.

"Now that we have it, how do we use it?"

"If they use liquid nitrogen, there must be some insulated tubing here to that will fit that nozzle. It'll be thicker than regular rubber tubing."

BANG! BANG! BANG!

"Jake?"

"Yeah, we need to hurry. The door won't hold him for long. Let's find that tubing."

BANG! BANG!

They both ran through the aisles looking on the various shelves in the warehouse as large dents appeared on the metal door.

BANG! BANG! BANG!

CLANG!

"Jake I've found it!"

"Run back to the tank! The creature is in here!"

They both got back to the tank and Qazjix tossed the tubing to Jake. As Jake tried to attach the tube to the nozzle, the creature walked up and growled.

"I'll hold him off. You get that hose attached. YAAAAAHHHHHH!"

Qazjix charged forward and swung her double fist into the creature's jaw. It shrugged off the massive blow and responded by slashing his razor sharp claws at her face. Qazjix ducked and threw a right jab that bounced off the creature's midsection.

"Jake, you need to hurry," cried Qazjix as she slid left to avoid a kick from the creature.

"Just a couple more seconds," he replied, as he finally was able to thread the pipe connector onto the nozzle.

Jake turned with the hose, just as the creature swung at Qazjix. She jumped back, but his claws hacked across her abdomen leaving three bleeding parallel gouges.

"Uggghhhh," she cried.

"Out of the way!"

Qazjix dove under one of the storage shelves as Jake turned the nozzle on and sprayed the liquid nitrogen. S103 snarled as it turned toward Jake. From her prone position, She grabbed the creature around the legs. It slowed, but in an attempt to break free, S103 swung it's left claw at her shoulder, cutting her. As Jake continued to spray, gradually, the creature stopped moving before it toppled onto Qazjix. Grunting, she pushed the huge mass off her and crawled over to Jake.

"You stopped it Jake."

"We stopped it. If you hadn't grabbed the creature when you did, it would have killed me before the spray could take effect. How are you?"

"My wounds are minor. Is it dead?"

"Who knows, but it won't thaw out for a while. I pumped all that liquid nitrogen onto it. Let's get out of here."

"That sounds nice."

Jake and Qazjix stepped around the prone creature and walked outside.

"It's awfully dark. I wonder if it's about to rain?" said Qazjix.

Jake looked up.

"It's not clouds, look up."

Qazjix looked up to see a huge black warship hovering several hundred feet above the compound. The ship was so huge that it cast a shadow across the entire island. As they stared up at it, a small panel on the bottom of the ship opened and several small craft flew out. The ships fell into formation and circled around until they landed in the middle of the compound.

"Jake, what is going on?"

"I think we're about to find out."

Armed soldiers exited the crafts with rifles drawn and ran toward Jake and Qazjix who had both raised their hands. Jake started to speak, but the soldiers ignored them and ran into the warehouse. An older soldier, carrying two metallic silver cylinders walked over to Jake and Qazjix.

"These are two new atmosphere scrubbers. Take them and leave."

"But what has happened here?" asked Qazjix.

The man looked at Jake and then to Qazjix before replying.

"Ma'am we've had a terrible industrial accident here. It was a terrible accident. Do you understand?"

Before Qazjix could answer, Jake jumped in. "We understand. Thank you. We'll just be leaving."

"Good luck to you Captain Astro and to you Qazjix. I suggest you hurry and we don't need to speak of this again. Do I make myself clear?"

"As crystal," Jake replied.

Jake took Qazjix by the arm and they began walking down the hill toward the Obsidian. She waited until they were far enough away that they couldn't be overheard before speaking.

"What just happened?"

"We just had our life spared in return for our silence."

"You don't think..."

"I think that if we had given them any trouble at all, we would have been eliminated. Let's just get to the ship and get these installed."

"But, how did he know your name and how did he know what you needed?"

"I'll say this once and not repeat it. This was an 'off the books' operation. It wasn't a private research project. We were observed and spied on from the minute that we got this job."

Qazjix didn't say another word until after the two scrubbers were installed. After the installation, they walked onto the ship and took their places in the cockpit. The Obsidian rose as Qazjix activated the null gravity field and the rocket engines.

"Jake, how do they know we won't talk about this later?"

"Take a look out the viewport."

As Qazjix looked out, she saw the landing craft that held the soldiers enter back into the mother ship.

"What, I don't see anything?"

"Just wait and watch the compound."

For the next 30 seconds, Qazjix watched until the three buildings in the compound exploded into a huge fireball. As the fire died, Qazjix could see that nothing remained of the compound save for the fence that surrounded it.

"Now watch the mothership."

As she watched, a small white dot exited the ship and began a circular path downward.

"Follow the dot."

The dot circled further and further down until it hit the landing pad. As soon as it hit, another huge explosion occurred.

"Do see now why they let us go. Even if we talked, what could we show as proof? There's no facility, there's no landing pad. We're just not a threat to them and their agenda."

"But who are they?"

"That was an intergalactic government warship.

They don't sell those things off as surplus."

"You mean our government was running this kind of operation?"

"And probably worse. I've heard of operations like this. I'll bet they took that creature's body before they blew up the compound. It wouldn't surprise me if they've got 50 compounds scattered about working on the same thing."

"But why, we're at peace. We are not at war."

Jake looked out the view port for a minute before replying. "Not yet, but it appears that they are preparing for something. Come on, let's go home. There's always another job that needs to be done."

Ashley Sherer

Ashley Sherer

Jake Astro
and the
Wandering Ghosts

Ashley Sherer

"Jajin spaceport, this is Captain Jake Astro of the cargo ship Obsidian with a load of parts for the mining town there. Requesting permission to land."

The sound of static was the only reply from the subspace radio.

"I repeat. Jajin spaceport, this is Captain Astro of the cargo ship Obsidian. We're requesting permission to land."

Static continued to emanate from the radio.

"It doesn't sound like anyone's home, Captain. What do you want to do?" asked Mikja.

"Does the radar show any traffic that we could hit, 'Qazjix'?"

"You're a funny man, Captain. If I didn't know better, I'd think you like her better than me."

"I just want to keep you on your toes. She might decide that she likes space travel more than working on her archeology studies."

"What does she have that I don't?"

Jake just stared at his perplexed co-pilot and shook his head.

"If you have to ask, you don't need to know. Now, if we can get back to the task at hand, anything on the radar?"

"Pretty evasive answer if you ask me, but to answer your question, nothing on radar. The scope is absolutely clear."

"I'm not going to let some backwater spaceport that can't keep someone on duty all the time keep us up here. Prepare for landing," ordered Jake.

Mikja quickly entered the landing coordinates and commands into the ship's navigation computer. The null gravity field enveloped the ship while the rocket engines fired to slow the ship as it was pulled to the planet's surface. The ship tilted nearly upside down as it entered the planet's atmosphere, throwing Jake and Mikja against their safety harnesses.

"What's going on?" asked Mikja.

"Correcting for intense magnetic field interference," replied Jake.

The ship slowly righted itself, until coming to the previous horizontal position.

"Where did that come from, Captain?"

"Sensors are showing a highly charged magnetic field much closer to the planet's surface than on a normal planet."

"It would've been nice if someone warned us."

"I think I'll take it up with whoever is supposed to do the cursory research on our delivery locations," said Jake as he glared at Mikja.

"Sorry boss, my mistake. I guess I got wrapped up in a book about the intergalactic government's plan to sell large numbers of different species into slavery with an extra-dimensional race."

Jake shook his head.

"Do you really believe all those conspiracy theories are true?" asked Jake.

"The truth doesn't sell. It is high in supply, but low in demand."

"Nice quote, but you make my head hurt."

"Could be a government implant."

"Ok, I think what would help would be silence."

"No problem, Captain."

For the next 15 minutes, the ship descended in a controlled manner until coming to rest on the landing pad of the Jajin spaceport. Jake gazed out the cockpit at the deserted landscape around him. The spaceport lights were on, but not a person could be seen anywhere. It was an eerie contrast to most spaceports that were in constant frantic motion with ships and people coming and going.

"What do you think, Mikja?"

"I've never seen a spaceport so quiet, Captain. The people have probably been abducted."

Jake looked at his paranoid obsessed co-pilot and shook his head.

"Or just possibly, since this is such small spaceport, the only person on duty has decided to catch some sleep. Technically, we're not supposed to be here for another six hours."

Mikja just shrugged. "I guess that's possible."

"Come on, let's take a look around."

"Take your pistol."

"What?"

"Take your pistol. I have a feeling," implored Mikja.

As paranoid as Mikja could be, Jake learned to trust his co-pilot's instincts. He opened a compartment by his seat and pulled out his pistol.

"Happy?" asked Jake.

"No, but it'll do."

"Ok. Let's go."

Both pilot and co-pilot unbuckled from their seats

and walked down the exit ramp of the ship to the cold dry concrete of the landing pad. Faded paint and rusted equipment showed that this spaceport was not heavily used. Jake motioned to Mikja and they walked over to what appeared to be the hangar/control room. Jake reached out to open the door, but it wouldn't budge.

"Locked. How do you like that?" asked Jake in irritation.

BANG! BANG! BANG!

"HEY! ANYBODY IN THERE?" yelled Jake.

BANG! BANG! BANG!

"You're just going to hurt your hand, Captain."

"Too late," said Jake as he rubbed his fist.

"Should we bunk in the ship till morning?"

"Hell no. I'm not staying on this backwater outpost any longer than I have to. It's only half a mile walk, let's go into town."

"You're the captain."

As Jake and Mikja walked the moonlit road toward the town, a warm dusty wind blew up from behind them. When they reached the outskirts of town, a strange high-pitched howl filled the air.

"That's comforting," said Mikja.

"You wanted to come into town great 'captain of the stars'."

Whoever called this mining camp a town, had decidedly stretched the definition. The town as Jake could see it consisted of a single dirt street with buildings on both sides. Jake didn't want to mention it, but the howl that they heard earlier seemed to be getting closer.

"Does it not strike you as a little odd that in a mining town there is no one out on the streets? It's not that late, is it?" asked Mikja.

Jake checked his watch, which he had set to local time. Mikja was right. It was only 2300 hours. At the least, the town bar should still be filled with miners drinking up the day's profits or mourning the day's losses. He turned and was about to respond when he noticed movement in a window in a building to their left.

"Did you see-" Jake started.

"the movement in the building to our left?" finished his co-pilot.

"I think we should take your suggestion and bunk in the Obsidian."

"You don't have to tell me twice."

The men trekked back to the ship when a loud snarl filled the air from behind them. Jake and Mikja whirled around and saw a brown and black outline on four legs galloping toward them.

"Jake?"

Without hesitating, Jake drew his pistol from his

shoulder holster. As he extended his arm, the creature leapt at them mouth open and fangs bared.

BANG! BANG!

The force of the shots knocked the creature to the ground. It staggered, but picked itself up and crouched to jump again. Jake never gave it the chance.

BANG! BANG!

The creature's neck whipped backwards as the last two shots ripped through its skull, killing it instantly. Jake's hand shook as he put his pistol back into the holster. As his hand fell to his side, the street was flooded with light from every building in town. People rushed out into the street with a deafening cheer. The sea of people engulfed Jake and Mikja and picked them up and carried them up on their shoulders.

"What is going on?" yelled Mikja over the roar of the crowd.

"I don't know, but they don't seem to want to do us any harm."

The mob carried the two men into the local saloon and sat them by the bar. An old man with a face that had been weathered and cracked by time walked over to them.

"Stranger, you got here just in time and you were worth every penny."

"That's right, you tell him Mitch," cried a voice in the back.

"Before you and your lizard friend got here, we were in terror. Nobody was safe, but now that's changed," said the man they called Mitch.

Jake and Mikja exchanged glances.

"I don't want to sound ungrateful for all this, but what are you talking about?" asked Jake.

The crowd started to mutter to itself.

"No modesty needed here mister. Our new sheriff can be proud to walk the streets of Jajin."

"Sheriff?" said Jake and Mikja as they glanced at each other.

"And we the citizens of Jajin officially welcome you and your strange deputy," the bartender interjected, "Now everybody, drinks are on the house! Mary, set'em all up."

The crowd let out a roar before heading off to the various tables in the room. Several men and women slapped Jake on the back and shook both the men's hands as they started the celebration.

"Mitch is it?" asked Jake.

"Yes sir. Mitch Johansen. What can I do for you?"

"Can we three step outside for a minute? There are a few details I'd like to go over with you."

"Hey! Everybody, the new sheriff's taking me outside, but he's promised not to arrest me."

The crowd roared with laughter as a few of the rowdier patrons threw peanuts at the men as they walked out into the street.

"What can I do for you sheriff? Anything you need, you just call old Mitch."

"Well Mitch, I appreciate everything, but there's a slight problem."

"We don't have any problems now that you're here, sheriff."

"That's the problem, I'm not the sheriff."

Mitch's jaw dropped until he smiled.

"You got me good, sheriff. I didn't realize we were getting a deputy also with the deal, even if he is a bit odd looking."

"Mitch, listen to me. I'm Jake Astro. I'm the captain of the spaceship, Obsidian. It's parked at the spaceport. I was hired to bring in a load of equipment and this is my co-pilot Mikja."

"No, no, no," Mitch turned around and then turned back, "This is going to just kill everybody. After the old sheriff was killed by the ghosts-"

"Ghosts?" interrupted Mikja.

"-like the one that attacked you."

"Mitch, I don't know a lot, but that thing was flesh and blood. Just look at it."

The three men walked up to the body of the creature

that Jake had killed.

"That's not a ghost."

While they were talking, a strong desert wind blew through town. As the breeze touched the creature, it dissolved before the three men's eyes until it was completely gone.

"Tell me that wasn't a ghost, mister."

"Captain, did you see?" stuttered Mikja.

Jake just stood there.

"Ok, you know what. It doesn't matter. I'm no sheriff so if I can get my cargo unloaded, I'll be on my way."

"Mister I don't think you understand. We took up money. Hard earned money and they gave it to me to send off for a new sheriff. Mister, I know I haven't got the right to ask you this, but could you play sheriff just until the real one gets here? If you don't I'll get strung up. Please Mr. Astro."

"Mitch, you seem like a nice guy, but I don't know anything about being a sheriff."

"But you killed the ghost."

"I got lucky, I'm not that good of a shot," explained Jake.

Mikja nodded vigorously, until Jake elbowed him in the ribs.

"How about we make us a deal? I've got a share in

this mine. I'll give you half of everything I bring up, if you'll be the sheriff until the real one arrives."

"What kind of mine is it?"

"Electrum."

Jake raised an eyebrow. "And you'll give me half?"

"Captain, remember the ghosts?"

"Tell me about these ghosts," said Jake.

Mitch leaned up against the rail outside the bar.

"About two weeks ago, we just hit a big vein, I mean one of the biggest, if not the biggest vein of pure electrum I have ever seen. Everybody went to the saloon to celebrate. As we walked down main street, Joe Duncan shouted the he had seen a ghost. We all looked where he pointed and sure enough there was this white shape floating across the street."

Jake frowned and Mikja crossed his arms.

"I know, I know. But we saw it BEFORE we started drinking. Since then, we've seen them every night and people have been disappearing. I'm scared mister. We're all scared."

"What happened to the last sheriff?" asked Mikja.

Mitch looked toward the ground. "He's one of the ones who disappeared. That one hurt. He was my brother."

"I'm sorry Mitch, I really am. Give us a minute," said Jake as he and Mikja walked out of earshot.

"We need to get out of here," said Mikja.

"A half share of electrum, would be nice. They aren't any ghosts here, just a bunch of hard drinking miners."

"You're no sheriff. Plus, how do you explain that thing disappearing before our eyes?"

"Ok, that was weird. I'll give you that. Maybe it was some kind of rapid decomposition."

"You don't believe that for a second. And what about those disappearances?"

"A bunch of drunk miners go missing? I bet most of them wandered off into the desert and fell down an old mine shaft. Think of the half share of electrum," repeated Jake with a smile, "I'll let you be my deputy."

"This is crazy, and anything I think is crazy has to be crazy."

Jake just smiled.

"Ok, I'll be your deputy, Captain, uh, I mean Sheriff."

The two men walked back over to Mitch.

"After much careful consideration, we'll be happy to accept your offer," Jake extended his hand, which Mitch shook heartily.

"Thank you. It'll be worth it, I promise. Come with me, I'll show you your office and get you sworn in."

Mitch led Jake and Mikja to a small, gray, concrete-block building that served as the Sheriff's office.

"Let me unlock the door."

Mitch took a key from his pocket and opened the door. The three men walked into a small office with two wooden desks and a small one-man jail cell in the back. On one of the desks, lay a gold, metal badge.

"Raise your right hand."

Jake raised his right hand as Mikja stifled a chuckle.

"Do you solemnly swear to uphold the laws and statutes of the township of Jajin?"

"I do," said Jake.

Mitch picked up the badge and pinned it on Jake's shirt.

"Congratulations, you are now the official sheriff of Jajin. As sheriff, you have the power to deputize your little lizard friend here."

"Don't I get a badge?"

"Sorry, fella we've only got the one. I can let you have this."

Mitch opened the topside drawer of the desk and pulled out a pistol and holster.

"That'll do," said Mikja taking the weapon and holster from Mitch.

"You know how to use that cannon?" asked Jake.

"I'm sure I'll figure it out."

"Well, I'll let you two get to it. There are cots in the back. We'll get the cargo unloaded tomorrow morning."

"I had almost forgotten about the cargo. Yeah, just come by tomorrow and we'll offload it."

"Have a good night, Sheriff," said Mitch as he walked out of the building and closed the door behind him.

"You've gotten me into some interesting situations over the years Captain, but this has got to be the most insane one yet."

Jake went behind the desk and sat down.

"Sheriff Astro. I kind of like it," said Jake as he put up his feet on the desk. "Have a seat at your desk deputy," he continued.

Mikja sat down at his desk and propped his feet up.

"Maybe it won't be too bad. A half share of electrum will be nice."

Just as Mikja finished, a figure burst through the door of the sheriff's office.

"Sheriff, there's a ghost at the edge of town," he yelled.

"Show us," said Jake.

The man led Jake and Mikja down Main Street.

"There!" the man yelled as he pointed to a translucent figure floating down the street before running away into the night.

Jake and Mikja crept up to the figure. It was as if a man shaped cloud had floated down from the sky. The figure extended a ghostly tendril toward Jake who drew back. Just as it started to follow Jake, a dog belonging to one of the miner's ran up and barked at the figure. The figure changed direction and went near the dog who continued to bark. It reached down and touched the dog. If Jake hadn't seen it with his own eyes, he wouldn't have believed it. The dog shriveled up with a small cry and fell over dead. Then, as the figure almost seemed to become solid in form, it disappeared.

"Captain, uhh, Sheriff, that thing just killed the dog."

Jake knelt over the dog. It was just a husk of what it was when it had first run up and its skin was drawn tight. As he touched it, the dog dissolved into dust before their eyes.

"I think we've found out what happened to the missing miners, Captain."

"I think we're getting out of here right now."

Jake stood up and started walking back to his office.

"We can't. You took an oath," yelled Mikja.

"Watch me. Would you like to stay?"

"Yes, I mean no, I mean. I don't know, but do you think that anybody here can handle something like this."

Jake stopped cold in his tracks.

"That's not fair."

"But it's true. These people have no chance against whatever these things are."

Jake stood silent for a few seconds.

"I guess we can take a look. Perhaps we can talk to the townspeople and see if there's a pattern to these things."

"We've got the hand scanners back from the pawn shop in the ship. We might could use those and see if we can detect any kind of energy anomalies," offered Mikja.

"Sounds like we almost have a plan."

"Scary isn't it."

Jake and Mikja went back to the ship and gathered up the hand scanners before heading to the sheriff's office. As they walked back, Jake did a quick energy sweep of the area.

"Did you get anything, Sheriff?"

"I'm not going to get used to that. You can still call me Captain."

"Nah. Sheriff is more fun."

"To answer your question, I'm getting some really strange readings but over the entire area. It may be that the electrum is causing some interference. We'll take more readings tomorrow."

Jake and Mikja walked to the office and went to the backroom. True to his word, they found two cots awaiting them. Jake actually found them to be more comfortable than the chairs on the Obsidian and soon he had fallen asleep. Jake awoke the next morning to the sound of a knocking coming from the front door.

"Mikja, we have a visitor. Get up."

Jake climbed out of his cot as Mikja stretched. As he walked to the front door, he looked around the office and found it even more depressing in daylight than at night. Gray concrete block walls held up a tin roof that he suspected would leak as soon as the first rain came. Jake opened the door to find a tall gaunt man dressed all in brown, covered in dust.

"Good morning, Sheriff. That was my dog last night that got killed by that ghost. I want to know what you plan to do about it."

"Uh, Mister?"

"Janson, Reb."

"Mister Janson, I want you to know we're going to devote all our resources to finding out what happened to your dog."

"Where's the body?"

"We're holding it for an autopsy."

"I want to see it."

"I wish I could let you, but we feel that an autopsy will help us in figuring out what's been going on."

"We?"

"Good morning, I'm Deputy Mikja," said Mikja as he walked to the door and offered his hand.

"A lizard? This damn place gets stranger all the time," said Reb ignoring Mikja, "I got to get to work."

Reb turned around and walked off without saying another word.

"Friendly people we have here, Sheriff. And how exactly do we autopsy dust?"

"I couldn't tell him that his dog dissolved before our eyes. Do you want me to start a panic?"

"No, but-" Mikja started.

"Things are bad enough with the townspeople thinking that folks are just going missing. How bad would it get if they found out these ghosts are turning them to dust? Oh, and don't forget deputy, you're the reason I'm here. We could be on our way back if not for your sudden attack of conscience."

"Ok, ok. What do you want to do then?"

"We do like I said before. We investigate and see if we can find a pattern. Also while we're walking around, we'll use the scanner to see if anything shows up. What do you think?"

"Not a bad plan."

"So have you ever seen anything like it?" asked Jake.

"No and I've been racking my brain all night."

Jake stood up.

"Come on. We're not going to solve anything behind a desk."

"Where are we going?" asked Mikja.

"Who knows everything that goes on in a town like this?"

"The bartender," they both said at the same time.

Jake and Mikja walked out the door and into the street. As they strolled, the cries of "Hey sheriff!" and "Get'em yet?" filled their ears. The short walk brought them to the town saloon where a short balding man was behind the bar wiping down beer mugs.

"Good morning, Sheriff. Morning, Deputy."

"Good morning. I don't think I caught your name last night when we were in here."

"I'm Joe."

"Joe what?"

"Just Joe."

"Joe, we're trying to investigate these ghosts and see if there is a link to the miner disappearances. What do you think?" asked Mikja.

"Well Deputy it's like this. It was all going along real good. The mine wasn't making anybody rich, but my business was good if you know what I mean," Joe nudged Jake in the ribs and let out a huge laugh. Jake and Mikja just looked at each other.

Joe continued, "Then about a month ago the miners hit a big vein, but couldn't dig it out. They needed some special equipment. It stopped operations for a day or two. About that time, a few people started to go missing. Most everybody figured they got bored and wandered off and fell in one of the old shafts that are around here. It happens. Miners like to drink. Which is good for me."

"What about the previous sheriff?" interrupted Jake.

"Old Bill Johansen? He was a bit of a drinking man himself and one of the first ones to disappear."

"Now about these ghosts?" asked Mikja.

"I've never seen one. Just a bunch of superstitious miners in a remote desert town."

"Have the people always seen the ghosts here?"

"Naw. I reckon the sightings started about a month ago. You'd hear stories about this ghost or whatever would be seen floating around the mines and around town. I don't believe it."

"Are the ghosts only seen at certain times?" asked Mikja.

"As far as I know, only at night. Course that's when most of the drinking is done."

"I think we've got enough information. Thanks for all the help, Joe," said Jake as he motioned to Mikja it was time to go.

Jake and Mikja said their goodbyes and went back out into the street.

"What do you think?" asked Jake.

"This is an odd town and he seems dumb as a brick."

"I mean, what do you think about the information?"

"I don't know. We know the ghosts are real or at least there's something around here. You killed something our first night here and we saw something kill that dog."

"Did you notice anything odd about the ghost after it killed the dog?"

"What do you mean?" asked Mikja.

"I've been re-running it over and over in my mind. I could have sworn that the ghost became more solid after it killed the dog. It was almost like when we first saw the ghost it was completely without form and you could see through it. You couldn't tell where its outline was, but after the dog was killed you could start to make out edges."

"I didn't notice that, but did you catch that this started about the time the big vein of electrum was found?"

"That doesn't make sense. It's just an electrum mine. They find veins all the time," said Jake as he shook his head.

"True, but Joe said they couldn't mine this vein immediately. It needed special equipment."

"You think there's some connection between the two?"

"I think it might be more than coincidence," declared Mikja.

The rest of the day, Jake and Mikja went around interviewing the townspeople. As they talked with more people, Jake started to think that Mikja might be onto something with his theory about the vein having some part in all the mystery. Everyone they talked to agreed that the ghosts appeared right after the vein had been unearthed.

"The sun is starting to set. How do you want to handle this Captain, I mean Sheriff?"

"Why don't we get up on the roof of the sheriff's office? It'll give us a good view of the entire town. We should be able to see any of the ghosts if they come around tonight."

"That's not a bad idea, but what do we do if we actually see one of them?"

"One step at a time."

"You have no idea," countered Mikja.

"I have no idea," said Jake as he nodded his head.

After the sun had set and darkness fell across the town, Jake and Mikja took up watch on top of the

jail. For several hours things were fairly normal.
That is, drunks on the street, drunks passed out,
drunks going back and forth from the saloon. About
the time they were about to call it quits for the night,
Jake spotted something floating from outside of
town.

"Look, there," he said pointing toward the direction of
what he had seen.

They watched as it floated closer to town.

"Come on, let's get down there."

Jake and Mikja climbed down the exterior ladder into
the alley beside the jail. They ran to where they had
seen the spirit, but by the time they got there it was
gone.

"This is ridiculous. It was just here," griped Mikja.

"Over there!" yelled Jake as he pointed toward the
bank.

The apparition was floating along the street as one of
the town drunks stumbled close to it. Taking notice
of the drunk, the ghost drifted toward him.

"Hey you! Watch out! Run!" yelled Jake as he and
Mikja ran toward the man.

As they got closer, the man looked up and saw the
apparition. His eyes widened as the specter reached
for him and his mouth opened to scream, but no
sound came forth. When the thing touched him his
skin shriveled like a raisin. The ghost dropped the
man just as Jake and Mikja reached it. As before,
the body blew away as if it was made up of dust.

The creature turned and snarled at Jake and Mikja. It swung its left claw and caused the two men to stumble back. Before Jake could steady himself, the creature jumped on top of him knocking him down.

"Help me!" Jake yelled.

It raised its claw and was about to slash Jake's throat when Mikja drew his gun and fired three shots into the creature's back. As the bullets penetrated its flesh, the creature let out an inhuman scream and fell over on top of Jake.

"Are you ok? Captain? Are you ok?" Mikja yelled as he ran and knelt beside him.

Jake tried to push the creature off him. As the rest of them had done, the creature dissolved into nothingness. He sat up and looked at Mikja.

"Did you see it?"

"Yeah, it nearly killed you. You're welcome by the way."

"Thank you, oh great green savior of mine. Happy? Now back to business."

"Yes, now I'm happy. Back to business."

Jake extended his hand and Mikja helped him to his feet.

"Back to the question. Did you see it?" asked Jake as he brushed himself off.

"What do you mean?"

"As it touched that guy, it got more solid. These things are ghostly, but as they touch something, it absorbs their substance or energy or something. That's how the bullets can kill it," explained Jake.

"Good job boss. How does that help us?"

"I have no idea."

"We are so messed up," Mikja chuckled.

"Hey, it was your idea to stay here."

"Don't remind me. Ok, so what now?" Mikja asked.

"I can't help but think this is somehow related to the mine and that vein they uncovered. Let's get the scanner and take a walk down there."

"Tonight?"

"Yep."

"In the dark?"

"It's the best time."

"This better be worth it," said Mikja.

After grabbing the scanner from the office, Jake and Mikja took the short stroll north of town to the mine entrance. The night time service lights were on as Jake and Mikja approached the chain link fence that surrounded the entrance.

"What do we do now boss? The fence is locked."

Jake pulled out a large key ring from his pocket and

found a particular key on the ring. He used it to unlock the padlock on the gate.

"Nice," said Mikja with admiration.

"The perks of being sheriff."

Once inside the gate, Jake resumed the scanning of the area until entering the mine.

"Perhaps we shouldn't go in there, seeing how we don't have a clue where to go," warned Mikja.

"Point taken, but I think we can go a little further than the front entrance."

"I wanted to bring bread crumbs, but NO, you said we wouldn't need them."

"You're not very funny."

"I think I'm hilarious."

"Come on," said Jake.

The entrance was hewn roughly out of rock and was about ten feet wide and seven feet tall. Every 20 feet workmen had installed electric torches to illuminate the shaft.

"Any idea where this vein is?" asked Mikja.

"Joe told me that we'll come to a fork in the main tunnel. We take the tunnel on the left. We'll walk another 50 yards or so and then there will be another fork. Then we take the right one. That will lead us straight to the vein they found."

"You mean it will lead us straight to getting lost."

"O ye of little faith. I'll use this," said Jake as he pulled out a small, white piece of chalk from his pocket.

"That's almost as good as breadcrumbs, Captain."

Jake and Mikja made their way through the mine with Jake marking their path with the chalk. The electric torches illuminated their way as they found the newly mined area where the vein had been exposed. Jake waved the scanner over the exposed vein of electrum.

"Wow!"

"What is it Captain?"

"I don't think I've seen readings like this ever, certainly not from just electrum. The energy signature is something very unusual."

"Captain, look at that!"

Mikja pointed to a spot eight feet down the mineshaft. The now familiar shape could be seen, floating in and out of the walls. As the shape went into the wall, the figure paused and then continued. Suddenly, a second figure joined the first and then a third.

"Do they not see us or do they not care?" asked Jake.

"I don't know. Captain, I'd suggest we exit and not press our luck."

"Agreed."

Jake and Mikja turned to exit, only to stop dead in their tracks.

"There's two more of those things and they're coming toward us."

"What do we do?"

Jake turned to see that the three original ghosts had drifted toward he and Mikja. The two men stood back to back as the five ghosts floated closer and closer.

"Pistols, and watch for the ricochet!"

Jake and Mikja took out their pistols fired into the floating figures. The bullets, however, went through the apparitions with no effect.

Click.

"I'm out, Captain."

Click.

"Me too."

The ghosts floated closer and closer as the two men stood back to back.

"I guess this is it."

"You know I probably should say something incredibly inspiring right now. Let's see. To Infinity and-"

"How can you get to infinity if it's infinite?"

interrupted Mikja.

"Fine math whiz, how about 'Not in the face'," suggested Jake.

"Inspirational, as always," said Mikja.

As the ghosts outstretched their arms, both men shut their eyes. For about 30 seconds, the two men stood still not saying a word.

"Captain, have you opened your eyes?"

"Nope, you?"

"Nope. Shouldn't something have happened by now?"

Jake opened his eyes.

"You can open your eyes, they're gone."

Mikja slowly opened his eyes and looked around.

"Where did they go and more importantly, why aren't we dead?" he asked.

"I don't have a clue, but I suggest we get out of here while we still can."

"And that's why you're the captain."

Jake and Mikja turned back the way they came and followed the chalk marks out of the mine.

"Hey, sun's up and it's bright," commented Mikja.

"How long do you think it's been up?"

"It's just over the horizon, so 15 minutes or so."

"Does that ring any bells in that lizard skull of yours?"

"No. Wait. That would be when those things would have disappeared."

Jake paced back and forth as he talked.

"So, we have ghosts that are somehow attracted to that electrum vein. They appear only at night and it looks like they disappear when the sun rises."

"They seem to get more solid as they touch something that's alive," added Mikja.

"Or more in this dimension?"

"You're thinking they're not ghosts at all."

"No, not ghosts at all. I think that electrum vein has caused some sort of dimensional rift."

"But why only at night?" asked Mikja.

"I don't know. Maybe it's temperature related or the change in how the solar winds hit the earth."

Mikja stopped in his tracks.

"It's not the solar winds. It's how the magnetic field changes when the solar winds aren't directly hitting it."

Jake stopped his pacing.

"The vein of electrum. Why is electrum so valuable?"

"It's conductivity properties, but I don't get it."

"This is a huge vein. One of the biggest ever seen, remember?"

Mikja nodded.

"Take a huge vein of superconductive material, add this planet's weird magnetic field and how that field changes at night when this side of the planet is facing away from the solar winds."

"A dimensional portal?"

"Bingo," said Jake, "but it's not quite on the same resonating frequency as our universe. These 'things' come through out of phase. When they touch something alive in our dimension they transfer energy, or mass, or a combination of both from the victim to the host. It makes them more 'real' in our dimension. That's why I could kill that first creature; it must have killed several people and was solid. That's also why we couldn't kill these. They had just come through."

"It makes sense, but how do we stop them?"

"I don't know. Yet."

"What do you want to do now?" asked Mikja.

"You head back to the office and handle any questions. I need to go to the Obsidian and run some numbers on the computer."

"Done."

Mikja exited out of the fence and started back to town. Jake took one last look down the mineshaft before he followed. As he walked toward the Obsidian, Jake saw the miners heading in for the day's work and wondered if his theory was correct. The trip to the Obsidian only took 10 minutes and he was soon sitting behind one of the computer terminals. After 20 minutes of research, his personal communicator beeped. Jake took it out of his pocket and pressed a button.

"What's up Mikja?"

"Captain, we may have trouble."

"What do you mean?"

"I talked with Joe. The miners are exposing the rest of the vein today in preparation of them digging it out tomorrow."

"That would be the worst thing they could do."

"What did you find out?"

"Apparently, the rock around the vein has provided some kind of insulation. As they continued exposing the vein, they eventually came to a tipping point that let these things come through. If they expose more of the vein, it'll be like pulling the stopper out of a bottle. These ghosts will flood us."

"That sounds bad."

"Now who's the master of the understatement?"

"Find the foreman and let him know I'm on my way."

Jake put the communicator back in his pocket and rushed out of the ship toward the mine. As he approached, he saw Mikja in an animated conversation with a man he assumed was the foreman.

"You don't understand. This will make things worse. These ghosts will overrun the town."

"No, you don't understand. I have a schedule and I have a bunch of angry miners that are waiting for the money that this vein is going to provide them. Do you know what would happen if I had to shut down the mining?"

The two men turned to Jake as he walked up.

"What my deputy is saying is absolutely true. I am ordering you as sheriff of this town to stop mining for the time being."

"Sheriff, if you want to go in the mine to tell my men to shut down, you go right ahead. But I'll tell you this; you probably won't come out under your own power."

Just as Jake was about to reply, a loud horn sounded.

"What's that?" asked Jake.

"That means that you're too late. It's the all clear blast."

As several miners ran out of the shaft, the lead one yelled, "Fire in the hole."

"Wait! Stop the blast!" yelled Jake.

A rumble could be heard from deep within the tunnel as the ground shook. A huge cloud of dust shot out of the mineshaft. For several minutes, Jake, Mikja and the foreman stood waiting for the dust to disperse.

"Well Mr. Sheriff, I don't see any ghosts."

"They only come out at night. You and your men need to get your families and and evacuate the town."

"I think we'll be ok. Why don't you just get back to being sheriff and let me worry about the mine."

"Come on Mikja, we've got about two hours to come up with something."

"What can we do?" asked Mikja as the two men left the mine and headed back toward town.

"I think we try to evacuate the town and pray that tonight goes by quickly."

"Where do we evacuate to?"

"What about the Obsidian? In a pinch, we could load everyone up in there."

"Yeah, that's right. Our cargo hold is empty now, but there can't be more than 100 people in the whole town. It'll be standing room only, but I think we can do it."

After they reached the town, Jake and Mikja started the near impossible task of trying to evacuate the townspeople. They split up, each man taking a side of the street. From building to building, they went warning everyone to be at the ship no later than sundown. In addition, Jake enlisted Joe the bartender to tell all his customers. Reactions ranged from disbelief and indifference to shock and concern. Several townspeople, especially mothers with children, were extremely frightened and went without argument to the ship. The sun was setting as Jake and Mikja regrouped on the front porch of the sheriff's office. They watched without a whisper, as small groups and individuals headed in one of two directions. They either headed to the Obsidian or they headed to the bar. Even Joe, while willing to spread the word, was unwilling to shut down.

"Think it's about time to head to the ship Captain?"

"I think so. We've given everybody a fair chance."

Jake nodded as he and Mikja headed down the road to the ship.

"How many people do you think will be up there?"

"I'd guess only 50 or 60. It's a little disappointing there aren't more. I hope that I'm mistaken about tonight."

"Captain, what we saw with our own eyes tells me that you aren't."

A large crowd milled around the Obsidian as Jake and Mikja arrived.

"I sure hope you're wrong sheriff. My husband told me to come here with the baby, but he wasn't going to be run out of town by any ghost," said one woman from the crowd.

"Ma'am, no one hopes that I'm wrong more than me," replied Jake.

A few other stragglers came up just after the sun went down.

"They're having a good time at the bar, sheriff. Joe said drinks are on the house if he sees a ghost," remarked one of the last few people to make it to the ship.

As the minutes passed and nothing happened, the people began to murmur amongst themselves. Several babies were crying and other children were heard whining that they were tired and ready to go home. Jake and Mikja scanned the town with binoculars searching for any sign of the ghosts.

"I don't see anything Captain. Do you?"

"Nope, looks like I might have miscalled this one."

"How long do we keep everybody up here?"

"Anyone can leave at anytime, but I'd stay till sunrise."

"Oh great," said Mikja sarcastically.

"What?"

"I think a dust storm is approaching the town."

Jake peered through his binoculars and saw a huge dust storm blowing toward the town. He wondered what else could go wrong until his eyes fell on the edge of the cloud.

"Get everybody in the ship."

"It's just a dust storm."

"That's no dust storm. Look at the edges and you can see what I'm talking about. That cloud is made up of the ghosts, thousands and thousands of ghosts. Get everybody in the ship, now."

Mikja announced everybody needed to load into the ship as Jake kept watch on the cloud. Within minutes, it had hit the outskirts of town. He watched in horror as the deadly wraiths engulfed building after building.

"Look! There's somebody running this way," cried a voice from behind Jake.

A man burst out of one of the buildings and ran toward the landing pad. It was almost as if his motion attracted the ghosts. He was swarmed by a cluster of the wraiths and was knocked to the ground. Within seconds, the creatures consumed his body energy and he dissolved into dust. The few people who were watching the process stood stunned. Jake and Mikja started pushing people onboard. With everybody loaded, Jake stood on the ramp watching the swarm. You could barely see the town for the mass of creatures. Jake's blood froze. At first he wasn't sure, but it appeared the cloud was growing larger. Jake ran into the ship and jumped into the pilot's seat. He activated the intercom system and made an announcement.

"This is the sheriff. Could I have everyone's attention? We're in no danger, but as a precaution we're going to lift off the ground. For everyone in the cargo hold, please sit down and interlock arms. Parents hold tight to your children. We'll have artificial gravity, but sometimes there are vibrations that can shake the ship. For anyone in a seat, please buckle up. Thank you for your cooperation."

Jake turned off the intercom and turned to Mikja.

"It's bad isn't it captain?"

"Yeah, it's coming this way. Activate the null gravity field. You can watch the external monitors, I've got the cameras pointed toward the town."

The ship crept upwards off the ground as the null gravity field caused it to vibrate.

"They're getting closer!"

"It's almost like they smell us."

"Give me full engines, we need to get above that cloud. I don't know if those things can fly and I don't want to find out."

The Obsidian climbed through the air, avoiding the rapidly approaching sea of the wraith-like creatures. Jake held his breath until the cloud, which had been getting larger and larger started to shrink. Much to his relief, it didn't appear that the creatures could fly much higher than 100 feet into the sky.

"Looks like we've made it out."

"I agree, set us in geosynchronous orbit over the town so we can monitor things. We'll set down when morning comes."

"Yes sir, Captain."

As the night hours passed, the colonists in the hold were quiet with few complaints. The mining life was a hard one and they were used to discomfort. Gradually, the rotation of the planet brought the sun breaking over the horizon.

"That is a welcome sight, Captain."

"I agree. Let's head back down, but keep us a couple of hundred feet in the air. If we see anything, be ready to give the engines full power."

"No problem."

Mikja engaged the null gravity field and the Obsidian descended through the atmosphere until hovering a few hundred feet off the ground.

"How's it look on the monitors, Captain?"

"I don't see sign of any movement. The town looks deserted."

"Should we set her down?"

"Yeah, but keep her systems fired up in case we need to take off again."

After Mikja landed the Obsidian back on the concrete pad, Jake turned on the intercom microphone.

"Folks, I'm going to ask you to be a little more patient with us. We're going to open the cargo bay doors to give you some more room, but we want you to stay close to the ship and not go into town until I can check everything out. Mikja is going to be at the controls and he can fly the ship back up, if any danger presents itself."

Jake flipped off the intercom and stood up.

"Are you sure you want me here on the ship instead of backing you up?"

"Not really, but I need you here in case we need to evacuate again. If something were to happen to both of us, these people wouldn't stand a chance," said Jake as he grabbed his pistol and shoulder holster.

"Here, take my pistol, also."

"Thanks, I might need it, in case any of our ghosts passed over to our side."

Jake took the pistol from Mikja and put it in the waistband of his pants.

As he walked down the ramp of the ship, Jake was stopped by one of the men.

"Hold up, I'm going with you, Sheriff."

"I won't stop you, but it'd be safer for you to stay here. I can't guarantee your safety."

"That doesn't matter. I'm going."

Jake nodded and the two men started walking in silence toward the town. It was shrouded in silence and not a soul could be seen walking the streets.

"This is my business here. I'm going in."

"Fine, I'm going to check out the bar."

The man walked into the building as Jake turned to go to the bar.

"Help! Help! Hel..."

The cries were coming from the building where the man had just walked in. Jake pulled his pistol and ran into the building. He scanned the room not seeing anyone until he peered behind an overturned table. The man, Jake realized that he didn't even know his name, laid there with his throat ripped out.

Creeeeeeeeeek.

Jake's blood went cold as he whirled around and beheld the creature before him. It was different than any of the creatures he had seen before. This one stood on two legs and was completely hairless with slits for eyes. Its skin was cream colored and when it opened its mouth it revealed a double row of razor sharp teeth. Blood dripped from its mouth as it chewed something. Jake assumed it had eaten the throat of the fallen man. The creature emitted a low guttural growl as if it was sizing up the new meal in front of him. Jake aimed his pistol as the creature crouched, but it jumped not at Jake, but sideways and started to run along the walls. Jake fired his weapon until it was empty as the creature jumped from the wall to the ceiling. Like a spider, the creature spun around Jake as he tried to get a bead on it. He remembered he had Mikja's pistol and reached to pull it out. As his arm moved to get out the weapon, the creature jumped from the wall straight at Jake. Jake ducked as the creature went over him. Before the creature could move again, he aimed and fired. The bullets ripped through its back

273

and knocked it to the ground. As Jake aimed at the creature's head, it looked up with an evil grin before it dissolved into dust. Jake slumped against a chair and caught his breath for a minute before covering the victim's body with a tarp and walked outside. He went into the bar unsure of what he would find. Chairs and tables were overturned, but there were no bodies anywhere. Jake peeked behind the bar, but saw nothing. As he exited, a shadow crossed into the corner of his eye. He whirled with his gun drawn.

"Don't shoot! Don't shoot!"

A shabbily dressed man in a yellow jumpsuit stood before him with his arms stretched toward the ceiling.

"Sheriff, am I glad to see you. I thought everyone was dead."

"Who are you and how did you survive?"

"My name is Jameson, Lars Jameson. I'm the electrician for the mine and the town. And as for your second question, I don't know how I survived."

"Tell me your story," Jake ordered.

"I was out at the substation, it's between the mine and the town up on the-"

"I've seen it," interrupted Jake.

"We'd had a few brownouts lately so I was checking out some wiring. That's when it happened."

"The ghosts?"

"Yes, I looked over my shoulder and thought we were in for a dust storm. Then the cloud got close enough for me to see what it really was. I was scared sheriff and I'm not ashamed to admit it. I dropped down and covered my head. After a few minutes and I wasn't dead, I took a look around. Sheriff, I don't know why, but they had bypassed me completely and had gone into town. They might call me a coward, but I stayed here 'til morning. I heard the screams from the town, but I couldn't move. I couldn't do anything, you've got to believe me."

"It's ok," said Jake putting his hand on Lars' shoulder, "I need you to show me where you were. It's important."

Lars nodded and motioned for Jake to follow him. The two men walked the short distance to the substation. The high voltage electrical equipment was enclosed in a chain metal fence. Lars opened the gate and walked to a spot near the center of the substation.

"I was right here and I got down like this," said Lars sitting down and covering his head with his hands.

"Ok, thanks. I really appreciate the help. You're welcome to head up to the Obsidian while I do a bit more scouting around."

"You don't have to tell me twice. Can I ask you something?"

"What?"

"Did anyone who stayed in town make it?"

Jake shook his head. "Not that I can see."

"I was afraid of that. Why did I make it, Sheriff?"

"Head on up to the Obsidian and I'll explain it to everyone soon. I need to finish my sweep of town."

Lars stood up and headed out of the fence and toward the landing pad. Jake stayed a few more minutes standing where Lars had indicated he had been. Shaking his head, he started off to the nearest building to sweep for survivors or creatures. Much to Jake's horror and relief he found neither in any of the other buildings. After checking the last building, he jogged out of town and up to the Obsidian. The crowd was eerily silent as he walked up.

"Is it as bad as I think it is?" asked Mikja after he walked up to Jake.

"Worse. I guess I better get this over with," replied Jake as he turned to the crowd.

"I need to make an announcement and I can't sugarcoat this," he announced to the crowd, "Other than Lars, there were no survivors."

Several shrieks and cries went through the crowd as the realization of the loss of husbands, fathers, and friends were hit home. This went on for several minutes until one voice in the crowd shouted, "Where's Bill?"

"Who?"

"The one who went off with you."

"He was attacked by one of the creatures. I'm sorry.

There wasn't anything I could do. Did he have family?"

"No, he was by himself and you didn't even know his name."

"We didn't talk. I'm sorry. I did stop the creature that killed him."

"Little consolation," said a different voice.

The crowd murmured at the announcement, but didn't offer to string Jake up, so he decided to continue.

"Now, I think I have a plan, but it will shut down the mine. I can't make that call, it's got to be up to you."

"We can't shut down the mine, it's our only way of makin' a living," cried one man in the group.

"Can't make a livin' if we ain't alive," answered a second man.

The crowd fell into three camps. One camp was in favor of the shutdown, the second camp was against it, and the third camp was apathetic to either choice. After about 30 minutes of discussion, Jake felt like he had to force the group to make a decision.

"I don't want to rush you, but if we don't have a decision we're going to have to go up in the Obsidian again."

Mikja came running out of the ship.

"Uh, captain. We've got a problem."

"No, there's no problem," Jake sighed as his shoulders slumped.

"Ok, then we've developed a challenge with the null gravity generator. We can't lift off until repairs have been made."

"And how long will that take?"

"About four hours, if we're lucky."

"We're never lucky. It's three hours until sundown."

Jake turned to the crowd.

"I hate to do this, but the decision has been made. The Obsidian is not going to be able to lift off again. If we get another flood of the ghosts like last night, we can't protect you. We have to shut it down."

The crowd started to grumble and a few cries came out.

"You have no right."

"What are we supposed to do? I can't feed my family unless that mine stays open!"

"Can you feed your family if you're dead?"

That seemed to quiet the crowd until one man spoke up.

"Ok, Sheriff. What do we need to do?"

"Can't we just blow up the mine entrance?" asked a man from the crowd.

"No, that's not going to be enough. These things would just float through the rock. The key is the electrum and the magnetic field of this planet, " answered Jake.

"Well, what's the solution?" asked another of the miners.

"If we run a big enough electrical charge through the electrum, it will turn into electrumite."

"Electrumite? Did you just make that word up?" asked Mikja.

"No, Sheriff's right. Electrumite is essentially burned out electrum. It doesn't conduct and it's worthless. I can run a cable from the substation," said Lars Jameson.

"Good, but we're going to need more juice than that. We're going to have to run a cable from the Obsidian as well. Someone needs to take a couple of men and run the cable. Then they need to drive metal spikes along the vein and attach the cable leads to the spikes. Mikja and I will run the cable from the Obsidian. Lars, do you have any extra cable?"

"Sure do, I'll get my assistant to bring over a spool."

"We've got three hours, I don't want to start a panic, but the rest of you might want to start off out into the desert. Maybe if our plan fails you can get far enough away to avoid detection by these things."

Jake had to give these people credit. They were a hearty, stern bunch. Lars quickly took charge and divided a few of the remaining men into three groups. Before they went off to their respective jobs,

Jake gave each group a communicator, so that the efforts could be coordinated. One group was in charge of driving the spikes along the edge of the seam, leaving a few inches exposed to allow the cable leads to be attached. The second group went off to the substation to run a spool of cable to the mine. The final third group followed the second group to bring a spool of cable to the Obsidian. Jake and Mikja grabbed the toolbox from the ship and started unbolting the plating around the null field generator.

"Do you think we have any chance at all?" asked Mikja.

"Nope."

"You going to tell them that?"

"Nope."

Before Mikja could offer a retort, a man driving a forklift pulled up. A spool of unwinding cable was trailing behind it. The man pulled the forklift up beside the open panel of the Obsidian and sat down the spool of wire.

"The end of this wire has been split and spliced off onto several feeder wires. When I left the ends were being tied around the spikes. They should be done by now," said Lar's assistant.

"Great, because we don't have a long time before the sun goes down."

Mikja took the end of the wire and attached it to the generator.

Beep. Beep.

Jake picked up the communicator.

"Go ahead."

"This is Lars at the mine. The spikes have been driven and cable leads have been attached."

"Great, I've not heard from the substation. Let me call them."

"Roger, just let us know if we need to do anything else."

"Will do. Substation, this is the Sheriff, what is your progress?"

The only reply on the communicator was static.

"Substation, this the Sheriff, what is your progress?"

Jake clipped the communicator to his belt.

"Let me take the forklift out to the substation. Their communicator might be malfunctioning."

Jake jumped on the forklift, backed it up and took off down the road through town heading for the substation. He gunned the engine until he thought the lift would overheat and breakdown. As he arrived, Jake peered through the chain length fence. No one was to be seen and it appeared than the leads had not been attached to the transformer.

"Hello?" Jake cried out.

The sound of the creaking fence door was the only response.

Jake walked through the door and looked around. As he stepped in, without thinking, his hand reached for his gun. An empty holster greeted him. Jake had laid the gun down on the toolbox so he wouldn't drop it as he helped unbolt the plating around the generator. Stepping around some of the large equipment, he brushed his hair as something dripped on him. His hand was red as he wiped his forehead. Jake looked up and stumbled as he saw the three men that had come to the generator had been hung from some of the guide wires around the substation. He started to crab walk backward away from the pooling blood.

Grrrrrrrrrrrllllll.

Jake froze momentarily before doing a forward roll. As he turned over, a massive claw came toward his face, smashing the ground beside him. Without thinking, Jake threw himself between four cement pillars holding up two electrical transformers. Without looking back, he ran to the opposite side of the substation. Once there, he turned his head only to see one of the wraiths leap toward him. Jake jumped to the side as the creature threw itself into the side of the fence with a massive crash. As it pulled itself up, Jake ran toward a circuit panel. He would have to time this maneuver just right. The deadly specter came around the corner to face Jake. As it jumped, Jake fell to the side, opening up the door to the circuit panel. A huge shower of sparks exploded out of the panel as the creature leapt into it. Bright spots filled Jake's vision as the creature twitched from the electricity that coursed through its body. After a few seconds, all that was left was a fine powder that dispersed into the wind. Jake staggered over to the panel and slammed the door shut. He then walked over to the leads of the cable and hooked them to the transformer. After the power switch was flipped, the transformer hummed as power flowed into the cables. Jake ran out to the forklift and grabbed his communicator.

"Throw the switch Mikja, the power is on here."

"It's done, Captain."

Jake ran to the mine.

A bright light could be seen from the mine. Jake looked back to the setting sun and then the mine. As the sun finally set behind the horizon, the glow from the mine faded.

"Did it work, Sheriff?" asked the mine foreman surrounded by his men.

"We'll see."

For several minutes, the men stood in silence until Jake spoke.

"I think we're ok, but I'm going in to be sure."

"If you don't mind, me and the boys would like to catch back up to our families."

"Sure, go ahead. Got a flashlight?"

"Here you go."

Jake shook his head as the men walked away laughing and slapping each other on the back. He turned to face the opening to the mine. Jake took a deep breath and stepped in. He followed the electrical cable that wound around to the exposed vein. He followed the spikes driven into the face of the wall. The light from his flashlight danced along the wall as Jake searched for any sign of the ghosts. Not seeing or hearing anything, Jake turned to leave. As he pivoted, something struck Jake in the back. The force of the blow threw Jake across the shaft into the opposite wall. Jake's eyes tried to focus as his back burned with pain. A blurry shape moved toward him. As the creature came into focus, Jake recoiled in what he saw. This one was badly misshapen and missing an arm. Its legs were bent backwards as it struggled to walk toward Jake. Jake looked around for anything that he could use to defend himself. Across the shaft, against the wall was a length of pipe. Jake front rolled across the room as the creature drew near. He picked up the pipe as the creature swung at Jake. Jake blocked the swing with the pipe, but was thrown backward by the force. The creature growled and started again toward Jake. This time he was ready. As the creature swung, Jake ducked. The creature's momentum turned it around and he swung the pipe at the creature's legs. It connected at the knees. The creature howled in pain as it fell to the ground. Jake raised the pipe as the creature kicked with his leg and struck him in the midsection. With the breath knocked out of him, Jake staggered back as the creature got back on its feet. The creature crouched and jumped, not at Jake, but against the shaft wall. With unbelievable speed, it bounced off the wall and toward Jake. Instinctively, Jake ducked as the creature flew over him. As he stood, Jake tripped over his own feet and fell against the shaft wall. His back to the wall, the creature bounded against the ceiling and hurled itself at Jake. Jake braced the pipe against the wall and covered his head. The creature slammed up against the pipe.

Jake slowly moved his arm and uncovered his head.
The pipe had impaled the creature through its chest.
The creature let out a small growl before going limp.
As with all the other creatures, it dissolved into a
fine dust as Jake watched.

"Hey Captain, you in here?"

The familiar voice of his co-pilot shook Jake out of
his stupor.

"I'm here."

Mikja walked up and stood over him.

"You look bad."

"Thanks, help me up."

Mikja extended his hand and pulled Jake to his feet.

"What do I owe the pleasure of your visit?" asked
Jake

"I noticed you left your pistol at the ship and I
wanted to bring it to you."

"Have you ever heard the old saying 'A day late and a
dollar short'?"

"I don't think so. What does it mean?"

"Help me out of this mine and I'll tell you."

Mikja put his arm underneath Jake's and the two
men started out of the mine and toward the
Obsidian.

Later the next day after a good night's sleep, Jake heard a voice calling out for him outside the ship. Mikja stepped near where Jake was sacked out.

"Looks like there's some people to see you Captain."

They walked out to a small crowd gathered around the ship. One of the men stepped out.

"Sheriff, we just wanted to thank you for all you've done. We know you're not really the sheriff we ordered and that makes what you did for us all the more incredible."

"I just hate I couldn't do more. Too many people have died."

"We know. It's going to take a lot of time for us to recover. But that's not why we came. We know you have to leave, but we wanted to give you this."

The crowd separated and a man with a box stepped forward. The man opened the box to reveal a large quantity of electrum.

"It's not a lot, but we wanted you to have it as thanks for saving us."

"It looks like there are several thousand credits worth of ore here," said Mikja.

Jake looked at Mikja.

"Look, I appreciate it, but we got paid for the cargo. You keep the ore. Use it to rebuild."

Several in the crowd started to cry as the spokesman from the group surprised Jake by giving him a tremendous bear hug.

"Uh, thanks," said Jake after the man let him go.

"We won't forget what you've done for us. Good luck and Godspeed," said another of the men.

Jake and Mikja turned and walked back into the ship. The two men sat in the cockpit and strapped in.

"What?" asked Jake as he turned to Mikja who stared at him.

"Sucker."

"Shut up and let's get out of here."

Jake Astro
will be back in
The Incredible Adventures of
Jake Astro
Volume II

www.ingramcontent.com/pod-product-compliance
Lightning Source LLC
Chambersburg PA
CBHW060544180626
46817CB00002B/721